The Morning Wood Tree

SIGGY SHADE

Trigger Warnings

The Morning Wood Tree contains the following content warnings:

Abduction
Anal sex
Blood drinking (menstrual)
Bondage
Dendrophobia (tree phobia)
Double penetration
Double vaginal penetration
Enema
Figging
Forced feeding
Forced lactation
Forced marriage
Forced pregnancy
Imprisonment

Nipple bondage
Lactation kink
Male pregnancy
Menstruation play
Nasophilia (nose sex)
Orgasm denial
Period sex
Perverted old grandpa
Pinnochio kink
Spanking
Water sports

To everyone who can't get enough of that sweet, sweet morning wood.

Chapter One

It's probably a bullshit old wives' tale, but I read somewhere online that it's bad luck to get your period on your wedding day.

Thank goodness for menstrual cups because no super-maximum tampon can hold back this flow.

I raise my leg to the ledge of the bathtub, fold the silicone in half, and ease it in. As I straighten, the cup settles into place and opens up to form a tiny vacuum. Relief floods my system, and I exhale the longest breath. The last thing I need on my wedding day is to worry about blood leaking through my gown.

A knock sounds on the bathroom door. "Are you ready, Milly?"

It's Clara, Erik's grandmother, who's been standing in for my parents. My heart aches with the usual pang of loss when I think about them, but I push away the sadness and focus on the happy day ahead.

"I'll be out in a minute, Clara," I reply.

"There's no rush," she says. "Erik is running a few minutes late."

I take a deep breath and wash my hands, making sure there's no trace of blood on my French manicure. When they're clean, I glance at my reflection and rearrange my ringlets.

The makeup artist has done a fantastic job and contoured my face to sharpen my rounded features. Erik made sure I hired the most popular professional in Stockholm, who has worked with the Crown Princess of Sweden. The colors bring out the highlights in my golden-brown ringlets and my eyes' aquamarine flecks.

My throat tightens. Mum and Dad would be so proud that I worked my way up through foster care and into the heart of one of Scandinavia's most eligible bachelors.

I'm wearing a bespoke Valentino gown with a Chantilly lace bodice that minimizes my huge boobs and cinches in my waist. Fortunately, the skirt is detachable, as is the ten-foot train, otherwise going to the bathroom would be impossible.

"Milly?" asks another voice. "Everything okay?"

I dry my hands and step out into the bedroom that's been mine since I moved into the Freyman farmhouse. It's a beautiful, three-story building that backs onto an ancient forest and has been my home for the past three months.

One of the designer's assistants attaches the skirt and train, while another attaches a tiara and a pair of heavy drop earrings encrusted with diamonds and pearls.

Clara clasps her hands to her chest and gasps. She's a tall, broad-shouldered blonde in her seventies with piercing blue eyes that remind me of Erik's. Today, she wears a pastel-blue suit to match the wedding's color scheme.

"You look like a princess," she says, her voice trembling. "I'm so proud Erik is marrying someone so healthy."

I smile, but my heart sinks.

Healthy?

Clara's accent is strong, but her English is even better than mine. There has to be a reason why she called me healthy instead of beautiful.

Before I can consider her words any further, she bursts into a flurry of Swedish too rapid for my mind to process, and another assistants attaches my veil. I can get a chance to take a final look in the mirror before she loops her arm through mine and marches me out into the hallway.

Her husband, Mikael, is waiting outside with his arms behind his back. He's in his late seventies with wrinkled skin and hair that's reduced to wisps of white.

I think he's ill. Nobody has actually told me directly, but Erik said he hasn't been the same since his great-grandmother died three months ago.

Mikael's features light up into a broad grin. "Milly, you look so radiant." His gaze falls on my cleavage. "The wedding dress is very flattering."

I shift uncomfortably on my feet. Erik's family has been unexpectedly warm and welcoming considering our whirlwind romance, but these compliments are a little backhanded.

None of this matters. Erik is expanding the family business into the UK and after the honeymoon, we're moving to a penthouse in London. Then it will be just the two of us, only visiting his family during the holidays.

Mikael clears his throat. It's a phlegmy rattle that only confirms my suspicions about his ill health. "Since you have no male relative to walk you down the aisle, may I do the honors?"

Guilt punches me in the heart for my earlier

thoughts, and I glance at Clara, who gives me an eager nod.

"Take up his offer," she says. "I'll be watching and smiling at you both in the chapel."

She disappears down the hallway, leaving me alone with her husband.

"Shall we?" Mikael offers me his elbow.

With a smile, I take his arm, my insides wavering between gratitude and discomfort. As we continue down the hallway, I can't help but notice the frailty in his steps. He isn't much older than his wife in years but there's a huge gulf between them in terms of health.

"When Erik brought you home, I was delighted," he murmurs, his breath labored.

"Oh?" I ask.

"You're exactly what this family needs. A new injection of life."

Mikael gives me a sidelong stare, his eyes so rheumy that I force my gaze straight ahead. I'm not sure what to make of his words. The Freyman family owns a significant amount of farmland in Sweden and is considered old money. I didn't realize any of this until I agreed to be Erik's wife, so no one can accuse me of being a gold digger.

I love Erik because he's exciting, funny, and has filled my life with non-stop adventure. If I had judged him based on his Tinder profile pictures, I would have written him off as an arrogant jock, but he wrote to me with the eloquence of a poet.

The fact that he's wealthy is just a bonus.

We pass gilded portraits of blond men and women in clothing from across the ages, their faces unsmiling and stern. From their chiseled features, it's obvious that they are Freyman ancestors. They each hold hunting rifles or the equivalent with the oldest carrying a crossbow.

I feel a little out of place, like a brown-haired interloper.

Anyone looking in from the outside can tell that I don't fit in, even though the family been so friendly. Everything was simpler when Erik and I were just dating. Now, it feels like I'm marrying into a legacy.

Mikael's steps falter, and he bends over double with hacking coughs.

My stomach flips. I grab his shoulder and ask, "Are you alright?"

"Water," he rasps.

"A-Alright."

I pick up my skirts and hurry down the hallway to the nearest door. All the guests who stayed over for the wedding should already be in the chapel, so I don't feel bad about barging into anyone's room.

Mikael's coughing picks up in volume, sounding like he's about to hack up both lungs. I open the nearest door and step inside.

There's a couple on the bed. The woman sits on the edge of the mattress and the man lies stretched out with his head resting on her lap.

Her large breasts are exposed and the man is sucking one of her nipples while the other is pinched between his fingers. I can't see her face because it's obscured by a curtain of blonde hair, but there's no mistaking the identity of the man.

Erik.

Shock freezes my limbs to the spot. The only thing moving is my stomach, which plummets to the wooden floorboards and shatters into tiny pieces.

I knew Erik was too good to be true.

Thirty-year-old millionaires with the body of a Norse god fall for athletes and supermodels, not curvy women who bake cakes. I knew all that but I listened to a soulmate meditation on Youtube and believed I manifested my perfect man.

"Erik?" I whisper.

He releases the woman's nipple, which dribbles with milk, and turns to meet my gaze.

"Milly," he says with a broad smile. "You look breathtaking."

My eyes widen at the man's audacity. It's one

thing to have a lactation kink, but how dare he cheat on me and not give a shit that he's been caught?

"Is it time for us to leave already?" The other woman raises her head and offers me a serene smile.

It's his mother.

I just caught my fiancé breastfeeding from his mother.

Chapter Two

Erik rises from his mother's lap, his lips still shining with her milk. His mother cocks her head to the side with a confused frown, as though I'm the strange one for gasping. I step backward, my stomach roiling, only to bump into Mikael.

The old man places his hands on my shoulders and grips them with surprising strength considering the poor state of his health.

"Are you alright, Milly?" Mikael murmurs into my ear.

"They..." I turn to meet his cloudy eyes, but the words die on my lips.

"Yes?" he asks.

I point toward my soon-to-be-ex fiancé. "Erik was...with his mum."

Mikael nods, seeming to understand. “My grandson has been feeding from his mother since he was a baby. It’s perfectly natural.”

My jaw drops. Does he know? How can anyone condone a grown man being treated like an infant?

Footsteps creek on the floorboards behind me, and my back stiffens. I can’t look at Erik. Not now. Not yet. I can’t believe he’s been kissing me this entire time and fully intended to kiss me as my husband with those milk-stained lips.

I can’t believe I had sex with a man who still feeds from his mother’s breast.

What in the Sigmund Freud? This is some Norman Bates-level weirdness.

What if I had children with Erik? Would his mother want to breastfeed them, too?

No.

No.

No.

That’s never going to happen.

Erik wraps his arms around my waist and pulls me into his broad chest. “It’s okay,” he whispers. “This is how things are with tight-knit families.”

My stomach roils with disgust. I may have been born to addicts and spent my formative years in foster care, but nobody gets to use my background as fodder for gaslighting.

"How long has this been going on?" I whisper.

"What do you mean?" he replies. "I've fed this way all my life."

I tear myself from Erik's grasp and shove him hard in the chest. "This isn't normal. This is not okay and you know it. All this time we spent together, you told me everything about your family except this."

Erik's brows furrow. "Milly—"

"No." I raise a palm. "You withheld this fetish of yours on purpose. I can't do this anymore."

"What are you saying?"

"I'm going back to London. Tell the guests whatever you want, but I can't marry a man who cheats on me with his own mother."

I turn on my heel, only for Mikael to block my way.

"You are not jilting my grandson," he says, his features as hard as granite.

All traces of the feeble old man are gone, replaced by the intimidating figure of a patriarch. He now stands as tall as Erik, yet four times as menacing.

Swallowing hard, I force myself to meet his eyes. "I can't marry him. Not after this."

Mikael turns his gaze toward Erik. "You told me this one was different."

Erik takes in a sharp breath. "Milly is open for anything. She's just shocked."

I whirl around. "What does that even mean?"

Erik jerks his head to the side, unable to look me in the eye. There's no sign of his mother, who I guess has disappeared into the ensuite bathroom.

It's Mikael who answers. "Erik was supposed to bring back a girl eager to continue the family tradition."

My lips part. I'm not sure whether I should ask, but Erik pulls me back into his chest.

"Don't worry about Milly," Erik mumbles. "I'm the most interesting thing that's ever happened to her. She just needs time."

The implication that I'm boring or my life was until I met him stings but not as painfully as this betrayal.

Mikael bares his yellowing teeth. "Time is running out."

I wriggle within Erik's grip, but his arms tighten around my waist.

"Don't anger Grandpa," he whispers into my ear.

"Let go." I elbow Erik in the ribs, making him grunt.

Mikael grabs my chin and forces my head up. "Erik could have proposed to a much better woman," he hisses. "More beautiful, better educated, with an actual pedigree, but he took a chance on a low-class dropout from the poorest borough of London."

I flinch. "Since I'm not good enough, then there's no reason for me to stay."

"You will not embarrass this family." Mikael's grip tightens. "You will smile through the ceremony like a dutiful fiancée, and we will discuss your options after we all return from the honeymoon."

A chill runs down my spine, and every fine hair on my body stands to attention.

"You're going with us?" I whisper, my guts hardening with dread.

Erik presses his body into mine. "If I spend too much time apart from Mother, then her milk will run dry. Since Father's also accompanying Mother, he will need to feed from Grandma."

I turn to Mikael. "Then who's going to breastfeed you?"

The old man's gaze drops to my cleavage.

Erik told me his family was close but I thought he was talking about warm hugs. When he flew over to London for our first date, he mentioned something about them also staying at the Dorchester.

Back then, I thought it was a nice coincidence. Now, everything he said about his relatives makes a sick sort of sense, starting from the grandfather's weakened condition. Mikael's health must have declined when his mother died, depriving him of breast milk.

That comment he made about time running out wasn't about the wedding. It was about him. He's failing fast without a source.

"Please don't tell me you expect me to feed you," I rasp.

"It's all part of the training," Mikael says, his eyes never leaving my breasts. "You will drink a tea made of lactation-inducing herbs, and I will stimulate the production of milk with a combination of hand expression and suction."

"What?" I whisper, my stomach curdling.

"It's natural," Erik says.

"I won't do it." My voice trembles. "If you make me go through the ceremony, I'll say no when the priest asks if I take you as my lawfully wedded husband."

Mikael's eyes flash. "Then you won't be leaving here alive."

The barrel of a gun presses against the back of my neck.

"You've given us no choice," Erik whispers. "If you don't go ahead with this wedding, then you will die."

My breath hitches, and my heart joins my

stomach on the floorboards. I can't let these people force me into a marriage I don't want, followed by an excruciating ordeal with an old man who looks fit to drain me of my youth.

Mikael steps closer. "Don't think of screaming for help. Every guest at the wedding is either a close friend or an associate. Nobody will believe the incoherent ramblings of an uneducated Englishwoman."

"Don't fight it," Erik says. "Just go through the wedding and lactation training. Once Grandpa's health improves and I find your replacement, we'll set you up with a nice divorce settlement."

I clutch at my chest, trying to breathe with the weight of their words crushing my lungs. These people are unreasonable. Crazy. And now potentially murderous. If I don't agree, I'm dead. If I go along with this terrible plan, my last flicker of hope will die.

My eyes grow hot. I blink over and over, trying to force back the tears. This was supposed to be the turning point in a life of hunger, humiliation, and hardship. The hope of meeting a loving and protective soulmate pulled me through the hard times. Now, I'm being reduced to nothing but a body that can produce milk.

I have to say something, anything to make these people let me go.

"But there are milk banks," I stutter. "People donate their breast milk all the time—"

"It has to be from the source and with our medicinal herbs," Mikael snaps. "Now, get moving before I decide to drink your blood."

Erik gives my neck a gentle pat with the gun, and the backs of my eyes burn with tears.

I have never in my life felt more powerless.

"Fine," I rasp. "I'll do it."

Chapter Three

It's funny how quickly desire can turn to disdain. I no longer find Erik the least bit likable or attractive. Everything he told me was a lie, starting with his profile pictures. He posted images of a handsome, athletic man with a broad range of hobbies.

He failed to include the one of him suckling from his own mother. He also failed to mention being the youngest member of a family of parasites.

The chapel is a fancy barn conversion with cream walls, exposed beams, and rows of rustic wooden seats. Huge bouquets of wildflowers adds pops of color, but the danger I'm in outweighs the beauty.

My mind is tumbling through my priorities.

First, I need to stay alive.

Second, I need to keep that old man's hands off my body.

Third, I need to free myself from these monsters.

As much as I don't want to marry Erik, it looks like I don't have a choice. I need to play along with these psychos until I can escape.

Mikael leans into my side. "Ready, Milly?"

I give him a sharp nod and try to keep my steps even as he walks me down the aisle. The tiara on my head now feels like the edge of a guillotine, and the bodice of my gown a straight jacket.

"You should count yourself lucky," he murmurs.

"Why?"

"When my grandmother was getting married, she also tried to run, but my great-grandfather threatened to throw her into the carnivorous ash tree."

"How does that make me lucky?" I ask through gritted teeth.

"It's a slow and excruciating death," he replies with a half-shrug. "We at least did you the kindness of offering you a bullet through the head."

"How generous," I say.

"I'm going to enjoy sucking your teats," he growls. "Erik tells me they're even longer and thicker than his mother's."

"Why don't you feed from her?" I hiss. "Or your wife?"

Mikael chuckles. "They're both taken. On a serious note, their milk is attuned to their sons. When we induce yours, it will be attuned to mine."

Fury simmers through my blood, burning away the last vestiges of my fear. The hatred I have for Erik pales in comparison to my loathing for Mikael. He isn't just going to feed from my body against my will. This sick bastard plans on enjoying my suffering.

The ceremony is a blur. I'm so focused on trying to escape that I don't hear Erik's vows. I don't flinch when the rings are exchanged, but cold sweat trickles down my back when the priest announces us man and wife.

"You may now kiss the bride."

Erik removes my veil and stares deep into my eyes before inching closer. Sour milk carries on his breath, making me gag. Bastard knows what he's doing. Before our dates, he always brushed his teeth and smelled minty fresh.

He grabs me by the back of the neck and leans in for a kiss. On instinct, I jerk my head to the side, and his lips land on my cheek.

Nervous chuckles erupt from the guests, accompanied by a smattering of applause. I've humiliated my husband, but I can't seem to care.

Mikael clears his throat and announces in

Swedish what I think means champagne will be served in the farmhouse, and the crowd rises.

Erik's fingers tighten around the back of my throat. He leans into me and snarls, "You shouldn't have done that."

My insides twist into painful knots. "Are you going to kill me?"

His eyes flash with something that mimics disappointment, and he releases his grip. "I thought you were different."

I wish I had a retort to put him and his family in their place, but no amount of scathing comebacks could ever fix this mess. The priest ushers us into a room at the back of the barn, mentioning something about signing a marriage certificate.

Erik wraps an arm around my waist and directs me to follow the priest. "Don't try anything stupid," he murmurs into my ear. "Sign the document to make our marriage legal and you won't get hurt."

"Why are you doing this?" I ask.

"You liked it when I sucked your tits. Your nipples are nearly as sensitive as your clit."

I flinch. "That's different."

"I will speak to Grandpa and ask him to be gentle."

"Did you even love me?" I ask.

Erik releases a long sigh as though I'm the one

being tiresome. "I like you. You're down to earth, submissive in bed, and fun. But I don't know you."

"So all that bullshit about not being able to live without me was a lie?"

"Grandpa won't live much longer without your help," he mutters.

The priest lets us into a small office containing a wooden desk and chair. He motions for me to sit, hands me a quill already dripping with ink, and slides over a piece of paper.

"Sign your name," he says in heavily accented English.

"It's in Swedish," I reply.

Erik's hand tightens on my shoulder. "It's a standard marriage certificate. Don't forget what we discussed earlier."

My gaze darts to the priest. He's a tall brown-haired man in his early fifties with an unsmiling face.

Erik leans into me and whispers, "Father Erland won't help you. Your only chance of leaving this marriage alive is to do as we say."

I stare at the paper, my body resisting.

"Sign," Erik says, his voice low and threatening.

"Alright." I move the quill to the certificate and scrawl my name on the dotted line.

Erik takes his quill and signs with a flourish.

Bile rises to the back of my throat. I'm officially married into a family of murderous freaks.

The priest exchanges a few words with Erik before congratulating me in English and leaving the room. As soon as the door clicks shut, Erik grabs my arm and hauls me to my feet.

"What are you doing? Let go of me!" I jerk my arm away.

He grabs me by the throat and walks me back to the door. "You owe me a proper kiss."

"No." I jerk my head to the side.

"Disobeying me already?" he snarls, his face a mask of cold fury.

He pins me to the door, his grip around my throat tightening. I claw at his fingers, trying to dislodge his hand, but he's too strong, too stubborn, too savage.

Sweat breaks out across my skin. My heart pounds so hard that it feels ready to burst. He knows I'm trapped, so he can take off the mask and show me the true monster beneath the handsome facade.

"Kiss me."

I need to do this so I can get the hell out of this room and plan my escape. My limbs tremble as he leans in and plants a kiss on my lips. It's cold and hard, just like the life I'll suffer if I continue with this sham of a marriage. My nostrils fill with the scent of sour milk, and I gag.

Erik pulls back with a smug grin. "Welcome to the family."

He reaches for me once more, and I skitter to the side, only for him to turn the door handle. "Now you can go."

I bolt through the exit and race through the barn, not looking back until I reach its double doors.

Erik stands at the far end of the building, staring after me like I'm his prey. I turn away and keep running down the path toward the farmhouse.

When I reach the door, I can't bring myself to enter. My legs keep going past it, even though I know I'll get caught and punished. There's no gun at my head or hands around my throat, but I still feel like a captive.

Erik's laughter follows me down the path. "Running already, Milly?"

I pick up my pace.

"We're surrounded by hectares of forests," he says through harsh chuckles. "If the lynxes and wolves and bears don't get you, I will."

The fine hairs on the back of my neck stand on end but my steps don't falter. I continue running through the wildflowers and to the start of the trees.

As I duck under the canopy of a huge oak, his voice drifts into the darkness.

"Hide, little Milly. We will enjoy the hunt."

This is futile. I say this to myself even as I tear off the train and step out of the skirt. Even if Erik returns to entertain the guests, he and his family are keen outdoor people. I'm no match for their hunting prowess but a girl's got to try.

I didn't endure shitty foster homes and I didn't dream of a better life only to become the human cow of a rich old man I despise. I need to escape, even if it means breaking my neck trying.

My feet carry me deeper into the woods. Light streams through the thickening canopy, barely illuminating the tangle of low shrubs and roots.

It's impossible to run in Vera Wang slippers but I'm not about to expose my bare feet to this rough terrain.

The plan is to continue for a few more minutes until I'm completely out of sight and then circle back toward the farmhouse. While everyone's getting drunk on champagne, I'll hide in one of the vehicles and hitchhike my way to the British embassy.

They'll issue me with a temporary passport, and I'll log into my PayPal account and buy a ticket back to London. If I can get a phone, I'll set up a gofundme and make a few posts on Tiktok. It's far-fetched but the best I can think of while my mind is still scrambled.

"It's better than nothing," I say through panting breaths.

An owl hoots, and my heart somersaults to the back of my throat. I glance over my shoulder only to find shadows shifting in the breeze.

Light shines in the distance from the farmhouse. I'm almost certain Erik is still standing outside the barn, watching my progress, so I quicken my pace. I duck under low branches, stumble over fallen logs, and flinch as foliage hits me in the face.

After a few minutes of running, the trees start to thin and the ground evens out, and I can barely feel the roots beneath my thin soles.

This feels like I'm on the edge of the forest. I break into a sprint and revel in a newfound surge of hope.

Until I hear a low, menacing growl.

My heart stutters, and I clutch at my chest.

Which animals did Erik say inhabited the forest? Lynxes, wolves, and bears?

I turn around again, only to lock gazes with three pairs of eyes. As they advance toward me, one of them walks into the light.

At first glance, they look like German shepherds,

only much larger and ten times as menacing. They have to be wolves.

I freeze, my breaths turning shallow, my limbs trembling. I can't fight, can't outrun them, can't do anything else but hope they get bored of staring at me and leave.

One of them inches closer with a tentative step. Without thinking about it, I raise my arms in the air, trying to make myself look larger and less like prey. The wolf pauses and cocks his head to the side.

Is it working?

"Back," snarls a deep voice that sounds like it's coming from the earth.

My stomach dips. What was that?

The wolves exchange glances before advancing toward me in a crouch, each looking ready to pounce.

Oh, shit.

An arm wraps around my waist and raises me off my feet, just as the wolf lunges. I scream, but something leathery wraps around the lower half of my face.

For a moment, I think it's Erik, but I lurch several feet in the air. I grab the arm only to feel bark. It's a branch.

"You may hunt all the animals in the forest but

one," the voice rumbles so deeply that the lining of my stomach trembles. "This human is my prey."

I rise higher and higher, over branches filled with rustling leaves until I'm at the height of the tallest tree. What I thought was the edge of the forest was actually the canopy of a tree so large that no other plant can thrive within its presence.

"Who's there?" I ask, my voice trembling.

The branch around my waist tightens. "Your presence has awakened me, and I hunger for blood."

"But who—"

"You chose the wrong time to trespass into my territory, human."

"The tree?" I rasp.

A low creaking of wood answers my question. I glance down to find an opening within the canopy.

That's when I remembered Mikael telling me that I'm lucky to have been threatened with a bullet through the head and not with the carnivorous tree.

Chapter Four

Terror grips me by the throat as I struggle within the grasp of the branch. No matter how much I thrash or scratch at its bark, the tree is immovable.

The wolves howl their protest from below as the tree continues lifting me above its canopy.

"Wait," I say, my voice trembling. "Put me down."

A deep rumbling laugh vibrates through the branch. "You would rather be torn apart by those beasts?"

"Than be eaten by a tree?" I shriek. "Please, let me go!"

"I hunger," he says, his voice as deep as wood scraping on wood. "And I must feed."

Cold wind blows across the top of the forest and over my sweat-soaked skin, chilling me to the marrow. My nostrils fill with the mingled scents of earth and leaves as the tree transports me to its center.

I inhale a deep, shuddering breath, trying to work out how to escape from this situation.

"L-listen, you don't want to eat me. I'm from a terrible pedigree. Wouldn't you like people of higher-born blood?"

The tree pauses.

My chest lightens with a spring of hope, urging me to continue spouting words. "I could bring you five delicious people. Five."

It rumbles, seeming to consider my proposal.

I squeeze my eyes shut and send a prayer to anyone listening that it works. All I have to do is wait a few hours for the wedding reception to end and for the family to begin its hunt. I could even scream a bit to create a trap.

Eventually, the tree groans. "Why would I risk losing the prey I caught when I do not need five?"

Shit.

The wolves continue howling, and I'm seriously considering joining them in their lament. If bribing this tree doesn't work then maybe I can negotiate a little mercy.

Before I can muster up something else to say, the branch carries me to a huge cavity at the tree's center. Light streams down from above, illuminating an unexpectedly empty interior.

Where are the bones, the rotting flesh, or the scraps of clothing from previous victims? There are no jagged teeth or probes—just empty space. That's not necessarily a good sign. Some carnivorous plants dissolve their victims.

Before I know it, vine-like appendages shoot out from the walls and wrap around my neck, my wrists, and ankles. I scream, but the sound echoes back through the cavity and rings through my ears.

I writhe against the restraints, my heart threatening to burst. More and more woody tendrils slip around my body, winding into the crevices of my clothes. Leaves sprout from the wood and tickle my skin with soft caresses, and one of them brushes against my nipple, infusing my skin with tingles.

This is unexpected. Not even Erik was this gentle.

With careful touches, the vines tear at the fabric of what's left of my gown. Fuck. I can't tell if the tree wants to bleed me or grope me. But at this rate, I'm going to die.

Strangely, I don't feel the obligatory blind panic. Maybe it's because Mikael already warned me of the carnivorous tree. Maybe it's because I've used up my daily quota of alarm, and my adrenal glands have run dry. That doesn't mean I don't fear for my life.

"H-how much blood do you need?" I rasp.

"One medium-sized human every century or so," the tree replies, its vine slipping into my knickers. "Why do you ask?"

"I know a way to give you blood and keep me alive."

"Explain," it says.

"P-put me down and release the vines first."

The branch around my waist deposits me on a hard floor covered in a thin layer of dirt. Warm air circulates across my skin, making it tingle. Is the tree trying to keep me comfortable?

I tilt my head up to the sky, trying to calculate the distance of the climb. Escaping this tree would be like trying to scale a four-story building that's determined to keep you inside. Impossible.

My brain had better conjure up an alternative way to feed the tree, otherwise breastfeeding Mikael will be the least of my problems.

"What if I fed you a little bit each day?" I ask.

"That would require staying awake," the tree replies, already sounding bored. "Better to consume you and sleep for another hundred years."

"And miss all the exciting things happening in this century?" I ask.

It hesitates again. "For example?"

"Did you know humans have discovered how to fly?"

"Nonsense," it replies with a scoff.

"It's true. They even sent some people to the moon."

"How do you know?"

"There's this thing called television. It's a bit complicated to explain to a tree."

It falls silent for a few moments, but the ground beneath the soles of my feet rumbles. I hope my attempt at reverse psychology works because I need to buy time to figure out how to escape.

A deep groan echoes through the cavity, sounding almost regretful.

"You will explain exactly how humans can fly to the moon."

"Of course, but it might take some time."

"Very well," it says. "And when you have completed the explanation, I will take your lifeblood."

My stomach plummets, and I clutch myself around the middle. I can't tell if it's dread I'm feeling or a cramp, but the pain only reconfirms my idea.

Erik and the others will hunt for me eventually. All I need to do is keep the tree fed until the others are in earshot and then lure them to their deaths. But first, I must ingratiate myself with the tree.

"May I offer you a little blood in the meantime?" I ask.

"I am incapable of taking small amounts."

Heat rises to my cheeks as I consider an alternative source of sustenance.

"I'm talking about menstrual blood."

The tree makes a pleased hum. "Show me."

Humiliation rushes through my veins, burning every inch of my skin with shame. I have never let anyone see me remove a tampon, let alone a menstrual cup, but this is a matter of life and death. With a groan, I lower myself into a squat.

"What are you doing?" it asks.

"There's something inside me that catches the blood."

I reach between my legs, but a branch slaps me on the hand. "Ouch."

"Allow me," the tree says, its voice low.

"Um... okay."

I continue squatting with my hands on my thighs and try not to tremble as a tendril the width of my forearm glides through the air, aiming straight for my sex.

"Wait." I rise and try to step back, but the branch returns to wrap around my waist. "That thing is too big."

"Hush."

The branch splits into five smaller tendrils, each with blunt tips. My breath turns shallow and I force myself to stay still. Is the tree making a hand?

Thick leaves sprout from the woody digits and part my folds with an unexpectedly gentle touch. A second pair of thick branches rise from the ground and wrap around my thighs.

The tree tilts me backward, so I'm lying suspended three feet from the floor and staring up through the cavity into the starlit sky. The view would be romantic if I wasn't in the clutches of a carnivorous plant.

"What are you doing?" I whisper.

"Making you comfortable so I can extract your blood-catcher," it rumbles.

"Oh, okay."

I expect the tree to plunge its wooden fingers into my passage, but its leaves brush over my clit with caresses that coax it to a state of gentle arousal.

More and more tendrils emerge from the ground, some covered in moss, others with lichen, but each rubbing over my skin. I throw my head back, relax into the soft touches, and surrender to my fate.

Sensation spreads through my core, down my thighs, and across my belly, and my nipples harden until they ache. Moisture slicks my folds and drips down my thighs. I can't believe I'm in the clutches of a carnivorous tree, letting it pleasure me with its foliage. My clit is so needy and swollen that I can't seem to care.

"Oh, fuck," I say through panting breaths.

"Are you alright?" the tree rumbles. "Tell me what you need."

My eyes roll to the back of my head. I'll be damned if I beg a tree for pleasure. "N-nothing."

"Then I will take my fill of your blood."

"A-alright."

I'm so hot and slick and wet that I barely feel the friction of wooden fingers sliding into my pussy and pushing against my inner walls. They clamp around the stem of the cup and give it a gentle tug.

It doesn't budge.

More wooden fingers slide into my pussy, trying to dislodge the cup. The tree explores around the silicone, pushing against a sensitive spot on my inner walls that makes them tighten.

"Fascinating," it says.

"Wh-what is?" I whisper.

"You are so responsive. I can tell how much you enjoy my touches."

"No, I don't."

"Your words may lie, but your body doesn't. You love this."

"Is that bad?"

"It is... different. Every human I have encountered has died in agony. You are the first to feel such pleasure."

Its fingers brush against that spot once more, making me moan.

"You like that?"

My eyes squeeze shut. Of course, I like it. At least my body does. This tree might want me dead but he's still doing a better job than any other man, including Erik.

Shit.

My mind can't keep up with what's happening. Maybe a powerful orgasm will release the tension, and I'll start thinking straight. Right now, getting pleasured by a tree is better than becoming its next meal.

The tree chortles. "You like this. Admit it."

"Fuck, yes."

I almost feel guilty for not telling the tree how to

get to the blood but I'm so close to the edge that I can't form complicated sentences. The tree continues to probe my pussy while rubbing the leaves back and forth against my swollen clit.

Pleasure builds up around my core. I gasp, arch my back, and spread my thighs, needing the tree to continue its sweet ministrations until I can climax.

The fingers increase their pressure and speed, seeming just as eager as I am to tumble over the precipice. I jerk and spasm within my restraints, begging over and over for release.

"Take your pleasure, little human," the tree rumbles.

Something inside me snaps like a broken twig, and waves and waves of sensation ripple through my core. I cry out, my voice echoing through the cavern.

The tree continues trying to remove the cup, its stiff fingers prolonging my pleasure until I collapse into my restraints, sighing, spent, and satisfied.

"What an interesting flavor," the tree says, its voice drifting through my consciousness.

"But you haven't reached my blood."

"Your slippery sap," it replies. "It is most refreshing."

Oh, fuck. It's talking about my fluids. All this time I was chasing my orgasm, when the tree was consuming my juices. I didn't think such a thing was possible with a menstrual cup but then I remember advanced level Biology. The Bartholin's glands that secrete lubrication are located at the entrance of the vagina, while the cup is halfway to my cervix.

A rumble spreads through the darkened space, followed by the words, “I want more.”

Chapter Five

The tree pulls the branch and its fingers out of my pussy, allowing me to catch my breath, even though I'm still suspended above the ground. My skin tingles with a tension that lingers in the air.

It's hard to explain. I'm inside the equivalent of the tree's belly, yet its gaze feels like a brand.

I can't give him any more. My body just wasn't built for multiple orgasms. Sex with Erik was good. He always made sure I climaxed, but it was nothing mind-blowing. I always found him to be more of a breast man than anything else, but I suppose it makes a sick sort of sense.

"You have stopped producing sap," the tree says, its voice heavy with accusation. "Where has it gone?"

It takes a moment to realize the tree probably

thinks I have two sets of veins—one that transports blood around my body and another one for vaginal secretions.

I clear my throat. "That isn't sap. It's a fluid women produce to get them ready for sex."

"Indeed?"

"If you want me to make more, you have to make me climax, but I can only do that once a day."

"Why?"

"I..."

The question makes me pause. People always say women are capable of multiple orgasms. My boss at the bakery never shuts up about how her husband can give her five or six climaxes a night, but I always thought she was talking bullshit.

"I've never had more than one orgasm. Most men lose interest after they've cum and don't care if I'm ready for another round."

"That sounds most unfulfilling," the tree replies. "Much like how I am feeling now."

I try not to flinch at the tree's barbed comment. Any unpleasantness and it might change its mind about wanting to keep me alive for long enough to lure my new husband and in-laws.

"Do you want to try again?" I ask.

"Tell me what you need to make more of that delicious sap."

I don't bother to correct a centuries-old tree but instead think of another way it can make me cum.

"Can you do suction?" I ask.

"I could hollow out one of my branches and harness the wind to create a vacuum."

"Uh… maybe not."

My mind drifts to the time I got off using the head of my shower. "How about a high-pressure flow of water?"

"That's possible."

It takes several moments to explain the concept of a shower and how a woman can use it to masturbate, but eventually, I make the tree understand. A branch emerges from the ground and thickens into a lotus seed pod, complete with tiny holes.

A second branch accompanies it that ends with a sausage-shaped tip that reminds me of a bullrush. Instead of hovering over me as the first one does, it floats between my spread legs.

"What's that for?" I ask.

"It's a porous seed head to soak in your sap while I drench you in mine."

"Alright."

The tree tilts me vertically, presumably so the makeshift shower can stimulate my clit without washing away my arousal. A shiver runs down my spine as I wait for it to start.

I'm now being held upright with my arms behind my back, my knees bent, and my ankles pressed into my ass. The restraints around my thighs pull them apart, exposing even more of my pussy.

"Are you ready for the plug?" it asks.

"Ready."

The bullrush-shaped branch tip nestles between my folds with back-and-forth movements. The coarse texture creates a delicious friction that reawakens my clit. As it drags over my sex, it absorbs all the wetness like a regular tampon.

The wooden shower head positions itself in front of my clit and lets out a trickle of warm liquid.

"Like this?" asks the tree.

"More pressure," I whisper.

The flow increases, and tiny jets of fluid pummel my clit. It's heavier and more slippery than water, making it even more intense.

"Better?" it rumbles.

"Fuck, yes," I reply with a groan.

The tree holds the branch in place, occasionally rotating and shifting the holes and alternating the water pressure.

"That's it." I buck my hips and writhe against the intensity. "More."

The flow increases, bringing me so close to orgasm that my breath hitches and my eyes roll in their sockets. Just as I'm about to climax, the water pressure recedes.

"What are you doing?" I shriek.

"You are producing copious amounts of delicious sap," the tree says. "I must keep you in this perpetual state of neediness."

"Why?" I cry.

The bullrush between my folds clenches and releases, seeming to pump my arousal into its branch. As soon as my pussy dries, the tree increases the water flow and builds me back up to a climax.

Sweat breaks out across my skin. I'm gasping, panting, and shaking. This is so peculiar. I'm being edged by a carnivorous tree and all I can think about is getting that orgasm.

"You taste so good," the tree rumbles. "Quite the delicacy. I cannot get enough."

Another climax builds. It's a slow, tingly feeling that makes my toes curl. Moonlight shines down from the gap in the canopy, and I release a breathy moan.

The pleasure is intense to the point of overwhelming, and I lose myself in the sensations. As the tree teases me to the brink and pulls back, I cry out.

A deep chuckle echoes through the cavity. I think my orgasm-deprived mind is playing tricks until the tree speaks.

"Patience, little human. You will be satisfied once I have taken my fill."

"Fuck," I rasp.

I'm a mess. This tree has reduced me to a mass of banked lust and unfulfilled desire. All thoughts from the outside evaporate into the ether. I no longer care that I'm a runaway bride hiding from a family of psychos—I just want to cum.

Hours pass, and the blood roaring between my ears drowns out the sounds of the forest. There could be a hunting party with guns and dogs, but I wouldn't hear a thing until the tree finishes its delicious torture.

The moonlight dims, but I'm too far gone to register the passage of time. My throat is hoarse and tears flow freely down my cheeks. I'm teetering on the edge of sanity and desperate for release.

As the first streams of sunlight seep into the void, the tree's branches shake me out of my stupor.

"You have pleased me, little human." Its voice echoes through my skull. "Now, you will enjoy your reward."

The water pressure intensifies, hitting my clit with jets more powerful than the ones he used when he was teasing me. When the orgasm finally hits, pleasure surges through my system like bolts of lightning, and my world explodes into a rain of sparks.

Spasms wrack my core, pushing the cup further down. I'm panting, thrashing, lost in the throes of ecstasy. The tree inserts two wooden fingers into my pussy, extracts the cup, and moves it out of sight. Then the digits return to stroke my g-spot.

It's as though every ounce of sensation that built up through the night is returning to burn me into ash.

"Oh, god," I scream.

"Correct," the tree says. "I am your god and I am pleased with your offering."

As my climax fades, every muscle in my body falls limp. A wooden platform rises from the floor, and the tree releases my restraints. I collapse into a bed of cool, springy moss, my limbs trembling.

For the first time in my twenty-two years of existence, I feel completely satisfied.

Wooden limbs part my legs and leaves part my folds. The tree inserts a fresh bullrush that nestles against my cervix.

"No more of those objects," it says. "From this moment forth, I will soak up your delicious blood."

"A-alright."

The mingled scents of lavender and chamomile flowers waft into the cavity, pulling me to a peaceful slumber.

I'm too exhausted to explain that a) periods only

last a few days, b) I plan on replacing myself with my in-laws before it ends, c) while the tree is eating them, I will escape.

As I fall asleep, I listen out for Erik and the others, wondering what's taking them so long. Shouldn't they have hunted me down by now? Shouldn't they be snatched up by the branches?

"Rest, little human," the tree rumbles. "For tomorrow, you will bring me more offerings."

Chapter Six

I awaken several hours later with sunlight streaming through my closed eyelids and piercing my dreams. The surface I'm sleeping on is warm and springy, with a soft pile that reminds me of a bed of moss.

It takes a moment for the memories to filter back in, along with their associated emotions. There's revulsion, both at the sight of my fiancé sucking his mother's breast and later forcing a kiss with those milk-scented lips.

Pain lances through my heart as I piece together how Erik set me up to feed his ailing grandfather. He never loved me—only the life force I could transfer to that evil old man.

I need to find a way back to London, where I can get this sham of a marriage annulled.

"You're awake," says a deep voice that seems to come from the earth.

My body goes rigid. Part of me hoped that I had followed my initial plan to hide in the forest and circle back to smuggle myself out of a guest's car. That I had fallen asleep in the back seat, ready to make my way to the British Embassy.

The stiff object pulsing in my pussy says otherwise.

Oh, shit.

I'm still in the clutches of that carnivorous tree.

Last night, it edged me to an inch of my sanity just so it could feed off my fluids. When it decided I'd had enough, the tree removed my menstrual cup and plugged me up with one of its branches.

Now, it wants my attention.

I read an article in a Sunday magazine about a lioness who had killed and eaten an antelope, only to adopt her child. The poor baby had no other choice but to follow the lioness around as its new parent.

The lioness took care of the baby antelope for a few days, seeming to treat it like a cub. Everyone thought this was cute and projected human emotions on the lioness. Perhaps she felt guilty for killing the baby's mother, they thought. Perhaps the baby had triggered the lioness's parental instincts.

No.

After digesting the adult prey, the lioness then proceeded to eat the baby. The lioness was just keeping the little antelope close for dessert, just like this tree is keeping me in its cavern for my blood.

"Did you sleep well?" the tree asks, its voice filled with warmth.

A gentle breeze floats over my skin like a caress. It threads through my hair with the touch of a lover and massages my scalp.

I will not be a baby antelope.

No. I want to be the photographer with the telephoto lens, watching the tree devour my husband and his shitty family of liars.

But for now, I need to act naive.

"Good morning," I say with a yawn.

"You are a most interesting little human," the tree says. "Did you know that you twitch when you sleep?"

"That's probably because I was dreaming," I sit up and stretch.

Sunlight warms my skin, making me realize that I'm naked. My gaze darts around the huge cavern. It's about twenty feet in diameter with a compacted earth floor and bark-covered walls that stretch up to the sky.

Now that the space is brightly illuminated, I can make out a few details. From the vertical lines that occur every few feet, it looks like someone planted a ring of trees that merged over time to form one gigantic plant.

Every so often, I catch glimpses of impressions in the barks. Some of them are intricate, like the symbols from Norse mythology, while others are runes.

"What do you dream about, little human?" the tree asks.

I take a deep breath, followed by another. Why is it trying to make conversation with its prey? My mind drifts back to why it decided to spare me in the first place. The tree was curious about the twenty-first century and wanted me to explain things like airplanes and rockets.

It's curious and bored.

I'll stay alive as long as I can keep it entertained.

"My dreams are filled with adventure," I say, remembering that cute animation I once watched on TV. "Like the time I visited Mount Draco to pet the dragons."

"What is a dragon?" the tree asks.

I rear back, my eyes going wide. "Don't you have them in your forest?"

"No."

"They're huge reptiles that fly."

"Like birds?"

"But the size of ten deer and covered in scales as tough as your bark, but I haven't told you the best part about dragons."

"What is it?" the tree asks, its voice breathy.

"They exhale fire."

The ground rumbles. "Impossible."

My heart skips a beat. I can't tell if this is a good sign or bad. Probably the latter, since fire can destroy plants. I'd better tone down my explanation so I don't end up becoming the messenger that delivers bad news and gets an arrow through the heart.

"It's true," I say. "But dragons don't come to Sweden. They live far, far away in the desert."

The ground stills. "That is good to know, but how can an animal create fire?"

I make up a load of bullshit and piece together everything I read about dragons from novels. The tree remains silent as I babble through a realm of fantastical pseudo-science until my stomach rumbles.

"You are hungry," the tree says.

My hand drifts to my belly. "I skipped my meals yesterday."

"Why?"

"I was nervous about my wedding."

"You are married?" it asks.

I nod.

"Yet you are not happy."

"My husband turned out to be a liar," I mutter.

Another rumble tears through my stomach, this one loud enough to echo across the cavern. It's more stress-induced irritable bowel syndrome than hunger, but I'm not about to explain that to a tree.

"You must eat," it says.

"If you could let me out for a few minutes, I can gather some roots and berries, then I'll come back and tell you all about the time a dragon let me ride its back," I say.

The tree doesn't answer.

"What about the time my friend and I hatched a dragon egg and the baby set his hut on fire?" I ask, my voice hopeful.

The tree shakes, filling my body with tremors.

I flinch. "Or maybe not?"

"Roots, berries, and what else?" it asks.

"Um... water and fruit?"

"Very well."

"Thank you," I say, a weight rising off my chest. "I'll be back as soon as I can."

I stretch my arms up, waiting for a branch to wrap around my waist and carry me through the canopy but nothing happens.

"Um... Excuse me?" I say.

Maybe the tree will open up a doorway through

the walls? I walk away from the bed of moss, only to feel a tug in my pussy.

How could I have forgotten about the bullrush the tree stuck in my vagina to soak up my blood?

Instead of a string, there's a thin branch that bends like a vine. I wrap my fingers around it and tug, only for the object lodged in my pussy to swell.

"What's this?" I ask.

"You will not remove my receptacle," says the tree.

"Then how will I gather food?" I ask.

The tree answers with a tremor, and a leathery sphere rises from the ground. It's about the size of a beach ball with multiple raised joints running down its sides.

I step back, wondering what on earth it could mean, only for the ball to split open and form a small picnic of oversized berries, tubers, and smaller leathery balls.

Clumps of moss grow close to the food, forming a low seat.

"Take as much sustenance as you need," the tree says.

Shit.

Lesson one. Next time I ask for food, don't specify what I want to eat and focus instead on getting let out.

"Wow, thank you," I say, injecting my voice with enthusiasm. "Could I eat that outside? I really want to see the rest of the forest."

The wall ahead of me creaks, creating an opening that's large enough for my head but too narrow for my shoulders. This fucking tree knows exactly what it's doing. It plans to pump me for entertainment and when I've finished, it will pump me for my blood.

"Eat."

I flop down on the cushion, grab a strawberry the size of a tomato, and take a bite. Flavor explodes on my tongue, making me moan.

"Good, isn't it?" the tree asks with a hint of pride.

"Delicious," I say through a mouthful of fruit. "I would love to see how it grows."

Before I know it, a large shrub rises from the ground, already laden with strawberries. I give the plant a side-eye. This tree is determined to keep me captive.

With a sigh, I pick up a small leather sphere the size of a tennis ball. It opens up to reveal a clear liquid that tastes like water, only sweeter and more acidic.

The tubers are bright pink and a cross between potatoes and carrots but taste like citrus. They should be delicious, but I'm too concerned about my immediate future to enjoy the food.

"Your blood has stopped," the tree says, its voice flat.

"Maybe it's the angle of my seat?" I shift to the side. "Is that better?"

The plug inside my pussy pulses.

"Give me more."

I grind my teeth and bite back a sarcastic remark. Where's Erik? What happened to his little hunting party and the promised retribution? I need those fuckers to start searching the forest so someone else can replace me as the tree's captive.

"Finish your food," the tree says, its voice clipped with impatience. "I wish to try something to increase your flow."

Chapter Seven

My heart sinks. Not just because the tree plans on taking my blood but because sensation rushes to my clit. I gulp down a mouthful of liquid and force down a rush of anticipation.

Last night was the most excruciating and satisfying experience of my life. The tree learned all my pleasure spots and teased them until I cried for mercy, only to deny me release. Then when I was about to pass out from sexual frustration, it gave me the orgasm of a century.

I can't allow myself to be drawn in by its sexual prowess. I can't become the baby gazelle, seeking comfort from a merciless lioness.

Taking a handful of the sweetest, juiciest blueberries, I pop them in my mouth one by one.

The air thickens, and the hairs on the back of my neck rise. It's watching, waiting, withholding its impatience. Erik used to joke about the best way to slaughter animals. His family believes that letting them die in misery and terror turns the meat sour. That's why they make sure to put the animal at ease before slitting its throat.

Fuck, I was so blinded by his wealth and good looks that I overlooked that red flag. Now, I know what it's like to be an animal being fattened and coddled.

"I never told you about the moon," I say.

"Finish your food," the tree replies. "I will hear your story while I feed."

My tongue darts out to lick my lips. "But you're getting blood—"

"Not enough."

The plug in my pussy makes a strong pulse, infusing me with waves of pleasure. I drop the berries onto the picnic mat, my breath quickening.

This is so wrong. I should be terrified, but there's a part of me that wants a repeat of last night.

With a deep breath, I pick up the last leather ball and drain its contents.

"How will you make me bleed?" I ask.

"I will massage your belly and encourage the blood to flow faster," the tree replies.

"Will it hurt?" I whisper, my voice breathy.

"Only if that's what gives you pleasure," it says. "Do you enjoy pain?"

I shake my head. "Will you be gentle?"

"Of course," it replies with a growl.

My pussy squeezes around the plug, which throbs in response. I should be thinking of escaping, but I already have a plan.

Erik and the others will come searching for me. I'm certain of it because Mikael's life depends on forcing me to lactate. When they get close, I will trade my life for theirs.

"Let's do it," I murmur.

Before I can even rise off the cushion of moss, the tree wraps its branches around my wrist and ankles, then lifts me away from the picnic and toward another mossy cushion a little lower than the bed.

After laying me on my belly with my legs hanging down the sides and my head facing the wall, a pair of branches spread my thighs wide and expose my pussy.

"Excuse me," I squeak.

"Yes?"

"Could I please look out into the forest?"

"Of course."

A hole opens up in the wall at eye level,

stretching about six feet wide. I force back a surge of annoyance at how the tree is generous with its window once I'm secured with several shackles.

Outside, sunlight shines down through the tree's broad canopy, casting a dappled hue on a clearing of clover dotted with wildflowers. The scene stretches toward spindly saplings that border the rest of the forest.

"Are you ready?" the tree asks.

"Yes," I whisper.

Thick fingers rise from the platform and stroke my belly. Unlike the ones that probed my pussy, these have a covering of moss. Or rose petals.

It's hard to tell when they're out of sight.

Another set of fingers run up and down my back, making me melt into the furniture.

"How does that feel?" asks the tree.

"Good," I murmur. "But why do you care?"

"You are my guest until you have completed your stories," it says.

I purse my lips, force down a deep breath and push away a rush of annoyance. What is this, a twisted Scheherazade, starring Milly and the carnivorous tree? Like the famous storyteller, I need to keep talking.

"You're so good at this," I say, meaning every word.

"Thank you."

"It reminds me about the time I visited the moon."

The tree's fingers falter for a second before continuing its massage. It looks like I'm on the right track.

"Indeed?" it asks.

"Yeah. I had to go to another country to catch the rocket."

"Rocket?"

With as much bullshit as I can muster, I give a semi-garbled explanation of vehicular travel. I describe it as a boiler that produces steam, which propels the engines. It's not like a tree knows the difference.

"You're so interesting," it says.

"Really?" I reply.

People have called me many things, mostly negative and variations of boring. It shouldn't feel so good but hearing this makes my heart soar.

"Of course," the tree replies. "It's not just what you say but the way you make everything seem so vivid. You are a most fascinating story teller, and you have such a beautiful voice."

I pause, my mouth dropping open as his words register. He isn't just impressed by my description of modern inventions but by me.

Pride swells in my chest, filling my insides with warmth. It's silly to feel so touched by the compliments of a murderous tree, but no one has ever called me fascinating.

Throughout my rambling tale, the fingers make gentle circles over my belly. Leaves rise from the platform and brush against my clit.

"Oh," I whisper.

"You like that?" the tree asks.

"What is it?"

"Humans call it Angel's Hair Artemisia," it says. "You are very sensitive there, so I chose something soft."

Tiny hairs rise from the leaf and tickle my clit, making my walls clamp around the plug. I exhale a breathy moan. "It feels like velvet."

"Where else are you sensitive?" the tree asks.

My nipples harden and press into the moss.

"Ummm... nowhere else."

The platform beneath me shakes with a deep, rumbling chuckle. "I think I have found another point of pleasure. May I massage them?"

"My nipples?" I whisper.

"Yes."

"A-alright."

Two indentations form in the platform and expand to make space for my breasts. The moss moves back and forth to stroke the skin, while a pair of velvety fingers roll my nipples.

Pleasure shoots down to my clit, and I release a moan.

It looks like the tree wants more than just my blood.

"Please don't tease me like you did last night."

"How else will you provide me with that delicious sustenance?" it asks.

"Y-you could make me squirt."

"Tell me more." The leaf rubbing my clit clamps around it, making me gasp.

"K-keep going," I say with a moan.

"And the plug?" The tree asks, making it expand.

"Bigger." I gulp. "Please. And less absorbent?"

The tree pulls out the plug, leaving me empty and clamping around nothing.

"Wait—what are you doing?" I shriek.

"Patience, little human," it rumbles. "I am selecting a suitable replacement."

A branch rises from the floor ahead of me, obscuring my view of the forest. Its tip softens to form a bud, which then expands to the size and shape of an average penis. The wood gleams in the sunlight, looking so polished that I almost mistake it for stone.

"Is that to your liking?" the tree asks.

"Longer," I rasp. "Thicker, with a bulbous mushroom tip."

The tree's deep chuckle rumbles across my front, and the leaves caressing my clit tighten to form a cocoon. Every fine hair on it sways back and forth, each stroking my sensitive bundle of nerves.

A pleasant shudder runs down my spine and settles in my empty pussy. All thoughts of the tree wanting to murder me vanished, replaced by a desperate need for the wooden dildo.

Within a few heartbeats, the dildo transforms into a ten-inch toy.

I'm panting so hard that I can barely say the words. "It's perfect. Give it to me, please."

The branch rises in an arc over my head and circles my opening, making me buck my hips.

"Please," I whisper. "Stop teasing. I need your wooden cock."

"Eager little human. If you want this cock, then you must give me what I need."

He wants blood. And a little pussy juice. There's little I can do to speed up the flow apart from writhing around like I'm in heat.

The tree withdraws the dildo, and the last part of my dignity snaps. I grind my hips and press my belly into the massaging fingers, trying to encourage the flow.

This reminds me of the time I searched YouTube for massages to reduce cramps and fell down a rabbit hole of reflexology techniques to induce periods, pressure points, and ways to manually stimulate the womb to make it bleed faster.

The fingers press into my belly deeper, sending a gush of sensation into my pussy. Warm liquid trickles down my folds, while the leaves cocooning my clit forms a delicious vacuum.

I'm so aroused and wet and slick. With my wrists pinned to the platform, I can't even stroke myself to orgasm. And all I can do about it is groan.

"You are producing," the tree says.

"Is it enough?" I ask through panting breaths.

"It's a start."

A moan slips from my lips. "D-don't forget you're trying to make me squirt. That means you can't tease me."

"I await your instructions."

Of course. I shake the fog out of my head. "Stick that cock inside my pussy and stroke my g-spot."

"The sensitive patch?" it asks.

"Yes," I say with a moan.

The dildo hovering at my entrance presses all the way inside with a delicious stretch that makes me groan. I'm so needy and aroused that I tremble as it fills me to the hilt.

I expect the tree to shift the dildo's angle so it can reach my g-spot, but the wooden rod grows a pair of notches that press against it.

"Excellent," the tree says. "Now, you will squirt."

It doesn't even give me the chance to direct the movements. The tree knows exactly how much pressure to apply and how slowly it needs to slide that dildo in and out of my pussy to make my toes curl.

I rest my head on the mossy platform and pant through parted lips. Today is more intense than yesterday's teasing because of the fingers squeezing, pulling, and rolling my nipples.

The only thing I need to make this scene complete is a dildo in my mouth and another in my ass. I force back that thought and focus on the plan to keep the tree entertained until the family comes hunting.

Pleasure courses through my core as the dildo moves in and out with measured strokes. I push my hips backward to increase the friction and chase the first orgasm of the day.

"Good girl," the tree says. "You are producing sufficient amounts of blood and sap."

The praise makes my skin tingle, even though I should be horrified. It's impossible to feel fear or moral outrage when it's stimulating my nipples, pussy, and clit.

Back and forth, back and forth, the knots on the dildo drag against my g-spot. Each time my walls clamp around the wood, it fills my insides with bolts of pleasure.

I'm so close to the edge.

The tree seems to sense the start of my orgasm, presumably from all the practice from the night before. Instead of slowing, it continues at a steady pace, teasing me toward delicious oblivion.

"I'm gonna climax," I say between ragged breaths.

"Good," it replies. "Let it all out. Let me taste your delicious release."

Pressure builds until my walls contract around the dildo. The tree continues teasing that spot with back-and-forth strokes, while the leaf rubs my clit to the point that it feels twice its usual size.

An orgasm tears through me like a hurricane, making me gasp and thrash within my restraints. I scream through the sensations, my vision filling with sparks.

Warm liquid flows from my pussy, but it's a combination of my juices and blood. I collapse, my chest heaving, my heart galloping around its cage like it's trying to find an exit.

Any moment now, the tree will complain that I didn't squirt and make me start again. I can't wait.

Instead, it yanks the dildo out of my pussy and pulls me to my feet.

"What's wrong?" I ask.

"Intruders," the tree snarls. "And they're human."

Chapter Eight

By the time I turn toward the window, it's already shrunk to the size of a dinner plate. Enough to give me a glimpse of the forest but nowhere near enough for me to escape.

I tilt my head up toward the sky. "Who's out there?"

The tree makes an annoyed rumble. "See for yourself."

Light floods the cavern from my left, and I turn to find a hole no larger than my fist. I jog to the new opening and peer out.

Olivia and William, Erik's mother and father, walk across the clearing, holding shotguns. Olivia continues toward the trunk, but William pauses to pick up something from the floor.

"She was here," William says.

Olivia turns to her husband, who holds up my Vera Wang slipper.

"Hey," I whisper to the tree. "I have an idea."

"What is it?" it murmurs back.

"Why don't you drink their blood?"

The tree pauses as though there's something to think about. I place a hand over my chest to muffle my heartbeat.

"I would much rather drink yours," it says.

"Why?"

"It's different. Delicious and with a unique level of depth. The more I consume, the more I feel emotions. This is pleasing."

I grind my teeth. If that's supposed to be a compliment, the tree can stick it where the sun doesn't shine.

"Don't you want more of my delicious sap?" I ask.

"Of course," it says.

"Well, if you plan on taking all my blood, I won't be able to produce anymore."

"Nonsense."

"It's true. All this time we've been together, I've been able to get aroused because I knew these people would come and find me."

"You planned on convincing me to consume them instead of you?" the tree asks.

My eyes narrow. Does it sound hurt? Damn. If I tell the truth, he might switch up on me and drain my blood. I resist the urge to shake my head because what I do and say next is a matter of life and death.

"Listen, we're both living beings, right?"

"Correct."

"And we both want to survive?"

"Of course."

"What would you do if someone bigger and stronger threatened your branches with fire or an ax?"

"I would defend myself."

"But they're much bigger and stronger, like the King of Dragons that was making all the smaller dragons steal food," I say, bringing up a half-garbled story I told it hours ago.

The tree pauses, seeming to think about such an impossible situation. I turn back to the hole to find William and Olivia no longer in sight.

My heart sinks to the dirt floor, and I clap a hand over my mouth.

"Where have they gone?"

"West."

"Show me."

Another hole opens up a few feet away. I jog around the wall to observe Erik's parents. They walk slowly, moving their guns from left to right as though I might jump out of my hiding place. I exhale my relief in an outward breath and lean against the wall.

"So, how would you escape the fire?" I ask.

"I would offer the stronger being a few dead branches."

"Just like how I'm offering you my period blood. It's flowing out of me anyway, and I'm happy for you to take it, but if I have to give you my life, my body won't be able to produce any sap."

"I see." The words are tight, reminding me of how some men try to keep a stiff upper lip after they've been rejected.

Silence stretches out for several tense moments. There's little else I can add to my argument. The tree has to see reason otherwise, I'm dead.

William turns to Olivia and flicks his head toward a copse of trees in the distance. Olivia gives him a sharp nod, and they walk away.

My chest tightens, and my pulse quickens with the onset of panic. Who knows how long this tree will take to make a decision? By the time he agrees to eat them instead of me, they'll be gone.

I have to do something.

Now.

"What's wrong with you people?" I yell through the hole. "You're sick."

They both whirl around and point their guns at the tree.

"What are you doing, little human?" it asks.

I don't answer the tree. I'm too busy being angry. Angry with Olivia for being a woman in my position two decades ago and not warning me about my fate. Angry with William for not putting an end to this generational curse. Angry with the whole lot of that family for forcing me to marry into their depravity.

"Fuck the both of you!" I scream, my voice shrill.

Olivia's gun goes off, and a bullet flies in my general direction.

A branch flies down from above and pierces her through the chest. William unloads the rest of his gun's magazines into the tree, causing an explosion of wood chips. A root rises from the ground and skewers him through the crotch.

"You shouldn't have done that," the tree growls.

My heart spasms. I stiffen, waiting for the tree to lash out. It's my fault it got injured. Erik's parents would never have shot if I hadn't yelled.

"Sorry," I whisper.

"Why did you shout?" it asks.

"They're my enemies," I replies.

"They hurt you?"

"Not directly, but they were part of the group who caused me pain."

The ground rumbles. "Then they will not survive their punishment."

My tongue darts out to lick my dry lips. "Will you take their blood?"

"Now that I have tasted it, I cannot resist draining them of every drop."

"Then what happens?" I whisper, my gaze rising the length of the walls. If the tree falls asleep for a century after it feeds, I'll be trapped unless it allows me to leave.

"Then you will receive your punishment."

"Why?"

"They damaged my bark with their projectiles. That wouldn't have happened if you had kept quiet."

"But you didn't tell me not to—"

"Silence," it snaps.

My jaw clicks shut.

For the next several moments, I walk around in circles, trying to figure out what on earth I'm going to do next. My period is so heavy that tiny streams of blood flow down my inner thighs and onto the floor.

"What if I gave you more sap?" I ask.

The tree doesn't respond.

Shit.

It's determined to feast on my blood, even

though I gave it two full sacrifices. I don't know what else I can do except hope it gets indigestion.

By the time I return to the small hole in the wall, William's body lies submerged in the clover, with Olivia mostly untouched.

"What are you doing?" I whisper.

"Pulling these bodies into the ground and grinding them so their flesh will nourish my roots."

"Like fertilizer?" I rasp.

"Nutrients," the tree says. "They will decompose in a matter of hours."

I lean my head against the wall and stifle a groan. "Impressive. Is that what you plan on doing to me?"

A deep chuckle resounds across the floor. "You are a morsel that must be savored, not devoured."

My insides twist into several painful knots that stretch up to my lungs. Is this another way of telling me he's going to kill me softly?

Blood roars between my ears and spots dance before my eyes. Air reaches my windpipe before pushing its way out in a moan. I'm so disconcerted that I have to double over and grip the wall for balance.

The only thing that kept me going was the prospect of getting the tree to eat Erik's family and then setting me free. Now that hope is dashed, and I'll probably die just like his parents.

"How will you drain my blood?" I whisper, my hand over my heart.

"What do you mean?" the tree asks.

"You're going to kill me, right?"

"No."

My lips part, and I let out a shocked exhale. "But you said—"

"I no longer hunger for blood, but you will still be punished."

"How?" I whisper.

The floor trembles and the wall on my left bulges. I jog backward with both hands stretched out to protect my face.

"What's happening?" I yell over the rumbling.

"You will see."

My ass hits something soft. I turn around to find another raised platform, and a pair of branches rise from the floor and snake around my ankles. They wind up my calves, passing my knees, and make a slow descent up to my thighs.

Another set of branches grabs my shoulders and pushes me so I'm lying face-down on the surface. I push myself up to my elbows and stare over my shoulder.

The wall straight behind me continues to protrude. A huge shape forms from the wood, resembling the outline of a human. Two spots shine from beneath its surface, looking like a pair of glowing eyes.

If this was a horror movie, I would close my eyes and turn my head away from the TV screen. I might even clap both hands over my face, but I can't stop looking.

It looks like the tree is sculpting a seven-foot-tall mannequin, with broad shoulders and a muscular physique. I shift on the platform, but the branches twine around my legs and spread them further apart.

A draft brushes against my skin, which I didn't realize until now was coated with sweat. I continue watching, my heart pounding, as the wooden mannequin steps out from the confines of the wall.

His eyes snap open, and his gaze sweeps down my body, making me tremble within my restraints. I want to scream, but that's what earned me my impending punishment.

Sunlight shines down on the tree, illuminating tanned skin the same color as ash wood. The mannequin advances on me with a manic grin, his eyes glowing an iridescent shade of amber.

"Now, let the punishment commence."

Chapter Nine

The mannequin approaches me, his chest rising and falling with excited breaths. I crane my neck, taking in his bulging pecs, tight abs, and a huge trunk of a cock swinging between his legs.

A moan catches in my throat and travels down to my exposed pussy. What the fuck am I doing? I'm trapped within the cavity of a carnivorous tree, who's just fed on my parents-in-law, and has fashioned a body made of wood.

I'm in the worst trouble of my life, yet I still have time to admire his impressive dick.

"You find my appearance pleasing," the mannequin says.

"It's perfection," I reply between trembling breaths. "But I don't understand."

"Your blood has changed me irreparably."

"How?"

"I enjoyed killing those people."

"So?"

"I have never enjoyed a thing in my entire existence."

"Oh. But that's good, right?"

The mannequin stops between my spread legs. I can't see his face, no matter how much I try to twist around within my restraints.

"With pleasure comes pain," he snarls. "Those missiles hurt."

"Oh, shit." I squeeze my eyes shut and brace myself for agony.

A warm palm lands on my ass cheeks and runs a slow circle over my flesh. He doesn't feel entirely like wood. It's like he's covered in a thin layer of leather that's as pliable as human skin but it's a little rougher with gentle callouses.

My breath catches, and a shiver runs down my spine.

The mannequin chuckles. "You have been a very naughty girl."

"I'm sorry," I say, my voice breathy.

"You will be." He gives my ass cheek a gentle squeeze.

I bite down on my bottom lip, hoping this

punishment will be pleasurable. His fingers slide down the crease of my ass and circle my pucker.

My asshole clenches, and I inhale a sharp gasp. Will he slide his finger inside? I tilt my hips, trying to give him a hint of what I want, but the finger slides back up my tailbone.

"Humans are such simple creatures, yet so intricate," he rumbles. "Every inch of your form is a wonder."

"You can touch it if you like," I whisper.

"I want to explore the secrets of your body."

"Is that why you turned yourself into a man?"

"A simulacrum," he says.

I'm pretty sure that word means imitation based on its first three syllables. What's the point in asking when I'm tied to a piece of furniture with my ass and pussy on display? I should be focused on my continued vitality, not expanding my vocabulary.

"What are you going to do to me?" I ask.

"You will choose your punishment," the mannequin replies, his voice deep.

My mind flickers through every form of corporal correction a tree could dish out that doesn't result in death. Paddling, whipping, and caning all sound too painful for my alarmed state. My brain would only translate the sensations as agonizing.

"How about a spanking?" I squeak.

"I hoped you would ask for a figging, but I will oblige."

"Wait—what's that?"

The mannequin walks around into my line of sight. His cock is already fully erect and lifelike, with thick veins running along its shaft and a bulbous head that could stretch me beyond reason.

I gulp, my gaze flicking from his glowing eyes to the bead of pearlescent liquid balancing on its slit.

"Figging is a form of punishment where a piece of ginger is inserted into the anus." He holds out a root about half as thick as his cock.

"Does it hurt?" I whisper.

"There's a burning sensation, but the moment will pass."

"How do you know about this?" I ask. "A moment ago, you were a tree."

"I have lived thousands of years and seen all manner of lives from the mundane to the most depraved, which includes their punishments. Figging is the least painful."

"Let's do it."

My mouth forms the words before I consider whether figging is better than spanking. How bad can a ginger root hurt?

The mannequin remains by my side and peels the ginger with the edge of his thumb. As the peel falls to the ground and disappears into the root, I examine his fingers to find them transformed into sharp edges.

What in the Edward Scissorhands?

Before I know it, he's shaped the root into a butt plug that's tapered at one end and rounded at the other.

He parts my ass cheeks with his fingers, making sure to circle my hole once more. "I'm going to coat your insides with a thin layer of oil to ease the slide."

"A-alright," I say between panting breaths.

Warm, slippery liquid oozes out from his fingertip, and he works it into my anus with gentle, in-and-out strokes. His touch is lighter than I expected and comforting, almost like a massage with his thick finger stretching me open.

I relax into my restraints and moan.

He removes his fingers and rests its pad on my pucker. "Now, I will insert the root. If the burning becomes too intense, you will tell me, and I will cleanse your rectum with sap."

"Okay," I rasp.

"Ready?" he asks.

"Yes?"

He pushes the root in, letting it stretch my insides. Thanks to the oil, it's a smooth slide, and all I feel is the mild pleasure of being filled. It's cool at first. My ass is so slippery that I can't feel any of the chemicals that give the root its characteristic kick. Once the plug of ginger is all the way in, he rubs a gentle circle on my ass cheek.

Warmth radiates from the root, making me sigh.

"Do you like it?" he asks

"Surprisingly, I do."

"Do you know why you're being punished?"

"Ummm... for letting you get shot?"

"And?" he growls.

My nipples tighten. "And for making you feel pain?"

He leans into me, his lips brushing my ear. "And for making me feel emotions," he snarls. "Did you do it on purpose?"

"What are you talking about?"

"I can't kill you, no matter how delicious you are. All I want to do is keep you pleasured and safe."

"Then why am I tied up with a ginger root up my ass?"

He raises a hand and rubs circles on my behind. "Because you enjoy being spanked. Now, be a good girl and count them!"

His arm swings through the air and lands on my ass cheeks with a sting. Pain radiates across my flesh, and I clench my muscles. My rectum closes around the ginger root, triggering a burst of heat.

My back arches. "Oh fuck. That feels so good."

"Count them," he growls.

"One."

The second slap lands on my left cheek, delivering a delicious sting that travels straight to my clit. My arousal surges along with the sensation, and I lift my hips off the platform, my muscles trembling with anticipation.

"Two."

Each spank delivers a fresh wave of pleasure that intensifies until I'm so lost in sensations that I'm begging for more. Heat surges in my ass from the ginger root, which my brain registers as flames of ecstasy.

I'm sweating, panting, and twitching for his touch. My nipples are so tight that they hurt. The muscles of my pussy clench and release, desperate for that wooden cock.

Liquid flows freely down my thighs. I can't tell if it's perspiration, my period, my arousal, or the remnants of the oil, but I'm so desperate to orgasm that I don't care.

"Eight," I cry out. "P-please fuck me."

"You haven't earned it yet," he says and delivers another spank.

"Nine!"

He slides his callous fingertips up and down my

slit, creating the most obscene wet noises. I buck my hips, desperate for him to touch my clit.

"If I had known you would produce so much sap, I would have spanked you earlier."

"Fuck," I moan.

"One final spank and I will fill you with my cock."

Chapter Ten

The mannequin takes his time, stroking my ass and drawing out my anticipation. I'm clenching, quivering, craving to be filled, and each touch of his calloused hands infuses my system with sparks.

Dappled sunlight shines down through the treetop and dances on the contours of his muscles. The effect is so realistic that he would look human without all that wood grain.

None of that matters. Not when he's delaying my pleasure. I raise my hips, desperate for that final spank so I can get some satisfaction. Then he'll stretch me open with that huge, wooden dildo.

"Please," I whisper. "I need you."

His deep chuckle makes the air tremble. I think he's enjoying making me suffer. Somewhere in the back of my mind, my mind is waving red flags. He's a carnivorous tree. A carnivorous tree that just devoured William and Olivia. A carnivorous tree that just created a man made of wood. A carnivorous tree that just admitted he likes the way I taste.

None of this matters. I'm past the point of reason. I'm too far gone to care. I'll deal with those red flags later. All I want right now is that sweet relief.

His hand comes down hard on my ass, sending waves of pain that my body interprets as pleasure. My rectum clenches around the ginger root, infusing me with the most intense warmth.

These conflicting sensations are too much, and my clit swells to the point of pain. I arch, my lips parting with a scream. An orgasm builds in my core, needing just the smallest touch to push me over the edge.

"Good girl," the mannequin rumbles. "You took that spanking exceedingly well."

"Th-thank you."

"Now, you may have your reward."

"Please," I say with a moan.

The bindings around my legs push them further apart until my thighs quiver with the strain. A gust of air blows in through the holes in the trunk and swirls over my folds. Liquid streams down my inner thighs but doesn't pool where my knees rest on the platform. The thought of the tree soaking up my fluids makes my clit swell.

His finger circles my clit. I'm so sensitive that I can feel each grain of the wood as though they're raised fingertips. I'm still flushed from the ginger and so close to climaxing that sweat breaks out across my skin and my breath comes in shallow pants.

I need more speed and more pressure. Most of all I need that thick, mannequin cock.

"You must have enjoyed that spanking," the mannequin says. "I have never seen you produce so much sap."

"P-please," I whisper. "Just fuck me."

"Like this?"

He slides the wooden cock up and down my exposed sex, making sure to linger on my clit.

I buck my hips and bite down on my bottom lip, but it only makes me more aroused. "Yes," I say through clenched teeth. "Just like that."

The mannequin lines up the blunt tip of his cock at my entrance and grabs hold of my hip with a large hand. I push back, needing that penetration, but he gives me a tight squeeze.

"Wait for it," he growls.

A sob builds in the back of my throat. What's wrong with this fucking tree? I thought the whole point of creating a wooden man was to experience sex with a woman, not tease her to the point of insanity.

I don't voice my thoughts. That will only distract the tree and prolong my frustration. Instead, I curl my hands into fists and wait.

The mannequin pushes in slowly, inch by delicious inch, stretching my entrance until I moan. He's already thicker than Erik, who until recently was my best-endowed lover. Annoyance prickles my skin at the thought of that conniving bastard.

I clench around the ginger root for a distraction, and a burst of heat burns away all thoughts of my husband.

"Squeeze my cock again." The mannequin makes shallow thrusts, filling me with tiny jolts of pleasure.

I clamp my muscles around the cock, triggering a fresh burst of heat that makes us both moan.

"Is the ginger root too much?" he asks.

"It's alright," I say through panting breaths. "I can take it."

"That's my girl."

He rolls his hips, making his movements more fluid. I'm so slick and sensitive that the woodgrain bulging through his leather skin feels like a ribbed condom.

I moan, my head lolling to the side, my muscles

tensing in anticipation of that sweet release. The mannequin picks up speed, entering me to the hilt and pressing hard against my cervix.

The wood inside me expands at the tip to create a V shape that's wider at the tip and pushes against my walls.

"What are you doing?" I whisper.

"Filling you," he growls. "Your cunt is a work of art and I want to see how far it expands."

My heart flutters. "Oh."

Reverberations emanate from the cock as it widens and stretches my pussy until it feels like I'll split into segments like an orange. I've never experienced anything as intense as this, not even when Erik and I experimented with dildos.

I cry out as the wood presses down on my surrounding organs. Warmth flares from the ginger in my ass, filling my insides with liquid heat. My clit is so engorged with sensation that it feels twice its usual size, and my bladder feels so full that it's about to burst.

"W-wait," I say between gasps. "If you keep pushing down on me like that, I'll pee!"

"Let it flow. I want your blood, your sap, and your piss," the mannequin says and gives my ass another slap.

My bladder gives up trying to hold back and

releases its contents. Warmth and wetness seep down my thighs and soaks into the wooden platform.

The mannequin groans. "You look so beautiful, gushing with liquids and feeding me with delicious sustenance."

Right. Because trees need watering. This is so fucked up but that's something I can think about after my orgasm.

Just when I think the mannequin has stretched me to my limit, the texture of the wood forms knots.

"Wh-what's that?" I ask, my voice breathy.

"Something to give you extra pleasure."

The knots expand and contract deep in my pussy, and I imagine them as stumpy wooden cocks, each fucking their patch of wall. I lose count after twelve when one of them pummels my G-spot, and my mouth opens in a silent scream.

My body goes slack, and I collapse against the soft platform, powerless to do anything but take the intense sensations.

Sweat pours from my skin and soaks into the moss, which grows around my body like a time-lapse. I'm covered in cool vegetation, with tiny strands of it tickling my flesh.

A gentle tendril wraps around my clit, holding it in place, while soft leaves move back and forth along its quivering surface. Two more plants wind around my nipples and tease them with gentle tugs.

The mannequin holds my hips in place as my core quivers with the stirrings of an orgasm. All the oil has drained away from my poor asshole, leaving it feeling like it's hosting the second circle of hell.

I can't take it anymore.

I need that climax. Right now before I self-combust.

"Please," I cry out.

"Tell me what you want," the mannequin says.

"I need... I need to cum!"

The mannequin spreads open my asscheeks, pulls out the ginger, and replaces it with his finger. The spicy butt plug lands on the ground with a dull thud.

Warm water seeps into my anus, massaging its walls and releasing the intensity of the heat. My ass clenches. Did he just turn his finger into a fuel nozzle?

"I'm going to pull out my finger, and you will hold this fluid in your ass like a good girl," the mannequin says. "Can you do that for me?"

"Y-yes."

"Don't spill a drop."

I give him a shaky nod.

He withdraws the thick digit, making sure to add

a few extra ounces of water. I clench my asshole, wanting to show the mannequin that I can handle the pressure.

The knots in his cock stop expanding and contracting and now make circling motions like a massage gun. Pleasure builds and builds until my entire body feels like a raw nerve. I can't hold back, especially not when the tendril around my clit increases speed.

I lie on the platform, twitching and convulsing, conflicted between holding the fluid in my ass and giving in to the pleasure.

The mannequin leans over my back, his lips brushing the shell of my ear. "You look so beautiful when you're holding back and trembling around my cock, but it's time to cum."

"But the liquid—"

"Let it go."

An orgasm blows through me like a hurricane, tearing through the last of my inhibitions. My asshole relaxes, letting out a flood of fluids. The walls of my pussy clench and spasm around the engorged cock and its knots, which continue massaging my insides.

All the pleasure escapes my body in a scream, pulling with it all my hurt and betrayal. This orgasm feels like being reborn into a new woman. One who can face down any of life's challenges.

Throughout this, the moss caresses my skin, and the mannequin wraps his arms around my body in a tight hug.

"You have pleased me," he rumbles. "You are a very good girl."

When it's over, I collapse onto the platform, my heart singing, my nerves thrumming with euphoria.

"Thank you," I whisper.

He gives me a gentle nip on the ear, his teeth wooden and blunt.

"Don't thank me yet. We have only just begun."

Chapter Eleven

I'm still collapsed in a pool of my own juices when the mannequin pulls back his knots and contracts his cock to form the shape of a cylinder.

My body relaxes with the aftershocks of my climax, and I exhale a shaky breath. Who knew that orgasms could be so cathartic?

Every guy I've ever slept with has promised to fuck my brains out but none of them have gotten close. The mannequin has far surpassed my expectations and has built me up with unshakable confidence.

If I can handle this tree, I can handle the problems ahead.

As much as I'm enjoying myself, this can't last

forever. The tree must let me go. I'll find my way back to London, file for divorce, and blackmail those bastards into giving me a hefty settlement.

The mannequin pulls out of me and helps me off the platform, his hands surprisingly gentle. I'm still basking in the afterglow, and feeling like I could sleep away the entire afternoon, but at some point, I need to leave the comfort of this cavern and face the world.

"Let's talk," I say.

He cocks his head to the side. "About the next phase?"

"What's going to happen?"

"I plan on giving you more pleasure."

"After my period ends." His wooden brow crinkles, so I elaborate. "I don't bleed like this all the time. In a few days, the blood will stop."

"I see."

"And you'll need to set me free."

His jaw tenses.

I place both hands on his chest. "You can't keep me here forever."

"I can."

"No."

He glares down at me with narrowed eyes.

"You like giving me pleasure, and I'm sure that's

because my menstrual blood has given you a spark of humanity."

"Yes?"

"I've enjoyed staying with you, but if you keep me against my will, I'll be miserable."

"But I know how to make you happy."

"It doesn't work like that."

"It can and it will," he growls.

Frustration wells in my chest, but I hold it down. The creature I'm talking to is an extension of an ancient tree that's spent hundreds of years exsanguinating people with no remorse. I can't expect him to suddenly develop compassion.

The more of my period blood he consumes, the more humanity he'll absorb. I just need to be patient.

"Why don't we discuss this again in a few more days?" I say with a smile. "In the meantime, I can tell you more stories. How about the time I found a golden ticket and won a trip to a chocolate factory?"

His features lighten, and his lips curl into a smile. "I always love hearing you speak."

"Do you need to stick a plug in my pussy to collect the blood?" I ask.

"No need." His cock lengthens and thickens, forming deliciously prominent veins.

Fuck. At this rate, I might never want to leave.

The mannequin lifts me off my feet and wraps my legs around his waist, letting me cling onto his shoulders and ride his dick. Throughout this, he gazes into my eyes with an intensity that fills my vision with light.

"What are you?" I ask.

"A being that is beginning to learn the meaning of life," he answers, his voice hoarse. "Entertain me with more of your delightful stories."

As I tell him about the impoverished childhood I spent picking up pennies to purchase a single bar of chocolate, his shaft drags against my g-spot, igniting my nerves with sparks of ecstasy and rekindling that last orgasm. Sweat breaks out across my skin, and every inch of my body feels like it's still infused with that ginger.

"And then... and then everyone in the chocolate factory screamed when he swelled like a blueberry... Oh."

"Tired already?" the mannequin asks, his voice playful.

"I'm a little unfit," I say with a laugh.

He walks us to the wall, where the bark is so smooth that it looks like leather, with a ledge that juts out to form a high seat.

After settling me onto the makeshift shelf, he

grabs my thighs and moves his hips. His thrusts are slow and deep, with movements that make my head spin. My story disappears, replaced by desperate moans.

I cling onto his shoulders, enjoying the tightening and contracting of his muscles. His body is a combination of wood and flesh that makes him feel like a statue that's come to life. Not just any old statue but a modern day Michelangelo's David.

"You feel so good," he growls as he pumps in and out of my pussy.

"Aaah!"

My heart thunders as he continues thrusting in and out of my wetness and driving me toward a peak. I'm so swollen and sensitive that I feel every ridge, every contour with an intensity that makes my eyes roll to the back of my head.

"You're tightening around my shaft," he growls. "But I want you to hold back your orgasm until I'm ready to spurt."

"Wait—trees can climax?" I rasp.

"I am a simulacrum."

"So, you're not the tree?"

"Something much more," he growls with a snap of his hips that pushes me even closer to the edge.

"Shit. I'm going to cum."

"Wait for it," he growls.

I clench my teeth, squeeze my eyes shut, and try to push my mind away from the pleasure. My thoughts drift to a future where I've returned to London and gotten back my job at the bakery, but it only makes my heart sink.

Weeks ago, I packed up all my things and left London, thinking I was moving on to better things. I still thought Erik was a minor executive within a firm that made herbal remedies and not its heir. I expected we'd have a comfortable life in Stockholm until he revealed the extent of his wealth.

I felt like Cinderella who had finally met her prince until the moment I caught him sucking on his mother's nipple.

My arousal recedes, but I don't feel any sense of heartbreak, just confusion. He could have joined a community of people who believe in adult breast-feeding, yet he chose me.

I'm so lost in my thoughts that I almost miss the mannequin's words.

"Nearly there," he says, his voice strained.

My eyes snap open, and I meet his glowing gaze. Sunlight shines down on his face, illuminating its perfect contours.

The tree has made a work of art with a masculine

chin, full lips, and a perfectly straight nose. His features are angular, almost regal, with a strong brow that frames his glowing eyes.

"Look at you," he says, his voice filled with wonder. "So passionate and hot. You're more beautiful than anything in the forest."

Warmth fills my heart and spreads through my insides, and it isn't even coming from remnants of the ginger root. Nobody ever described me in such superlative terms. I could bask in this admiration forever.

His cock swells, and the hands gripping my thighs tighten. A moss-covered knot rises from above his cock and strokes my clit, making me see stars.

"I'm going to fill you with my release," he growls. "And you're going to take every single drop."

Bloody hell.

The knot continues rubbing against my clit, while his cock strokes my insides until I'm so overwhelmed with pleasure that my muscles flutter.

"Do it, little human," the mannequin growls. "Cum with me."

Soft tendrils rise from the moss and slap my swollen clit, triggering a chain reaction that has me convulsing. The mannequin holds me steady through the orgasm but the sensations are so overwhelming that I'm only vaguely aware when he roars.

Spurts of warm liquid hit my walls until I become so full that it pours freely out of my pussy and onto the ledge.

He continues cumming, his roar sounding more like thunder than a voice. The base of his cock expands, forming a plug around my entrance and trapping all the fluids. A few heartbeats later, my pussy is stretched beyond reason.

I thought I felt full when he expanded his cock and pummeled me with his knots. That was nothing compared to the deluge of his release.

My walls continue to spasm through the orgasm. Instead of squeezing his shaft, they grasp a well of warm liquid.

"What a greedy little human," he rumbles. "Drawing out my sap. Would you like a taste?"

"Yes, please."

I expect the mannequin to pull out of my pussy, but his lips crash against mine. His tongue is softer than expected—more like thickened rose petals than wood. It explores my mouth with a desperate hunger that makes me moan.

"Here it comes," he mumbles around the kiss.

Warm fluid seeps into my mouth, tasting sweeter

than the liquid in the leather balls. It's a little like maple syrup with a hint of blossoms and honey.

I swallow several mouthfuls before pulling away, my belly close to bursting.

"That was delicious."

He grins. "I'm glad you enjoyed the taste, but I think you can take more."

Chapter Twelve

The mannequin fucks me in every position imaginable. With me lying face-down on the floor, held several feet in the air with my arms and legs suspended by branches, from behind while standing, and on all fours.

Each time he fills me with his sap until I'm overflowing, until I'm so wrung out and exhausted that I can barely support my own body.

By the time the last vestiges of sunlight stream down from the tree's opening, my legs give up, and my body collapses like a broken marionette. The mannequin catches me before I fall and cradles me in his strong arms.

"You are wilting," he says.

"Just tired," I reply with a yawn.

"Would you like sustenance?"

I huff a laugh and glance down at my belly.

"What is it?" he asks.

"Nobody could eat after consuming so much of your sap."

The mannequin smiles. "You're satisfied?"

"That's an understatement."

"Let's get you nice and clean."

A plug pushes its way into my pussy. I glance down and find a thin branch leading into his body, looking like he doesn't want to miss a drop of my period blood.

He carries me to the center of the cavern, where the ground hollows out to form a pool filled with bubbling water. Curls of steam rise from its surface, releasing the mingled scents of eucalyptus and mint.

"What's this?" I ask.

"I directed some groundwater from deep within the earth to form a bath," he replies. "Do you like it?"

"You did this for me?"

The mannequin pauses and looks me full in the face. "Of course. No one has made me feel so alive in my entire three-thousand years of existence."

My lips part, but I can't form any words. Why does he always makes me feel so appreciated? So special? He lets me talk for hours and hangs onto my every word. He showers me with compliments and praise. It's as though my blood has attuned his personality to my needs.

Wait. Three thousand years? I knew he was old, but this is beyond my expectations. Before I can muster up something to say, he steps down into the bath and lowers me into the warm water.

The liquid is smoother and more slippery than anything that comes out of the tap, and with bubbles that caress my skin. My muscles loosen, feeling like I'm in a spa.

"Did you have a name?" I whisper.

"Some called me the Tree of Life and others refer to me as the World Tree. Before then, I was known as Yggdrasil." He enunciates each syllable, producing the sound Ig-dra-zil with a rolled R.

"Is that Old Norse?" I ask.

Nodding, he tips me backward to soak my hair. Warm water caresses my scalp, along with several bubbles.

"Years ago, it was me who connected the nine worlds and conversed with the gods. It was I who soaked in the waters of the Well of Wisdom that enhanced Odin's intelligence in exchange for his eye."

My breath shallows, and I gaze into the mannequin's amber eyes. He's more than just an aspect of the carnivorous tree. He's practically a god.

"What would you like me to call you Yggdrasil?" I squeak.

"Something different," he answers with a smile. "I'm no longer that being."

"What happened?"

His lips tighten into a bitter smile. "Ragnarök."

I'm not the biggest Marvel fan but I've watched enough movies to know that he's talking about the Norse version of armageddon. Twenty-four hours ago, my entire life crumbled. I can't imagine what it's like to witness the destruction of an entire world.

"Do you want to talk about it?" I ask.

He shakes his head. "It was a long time ago, and I was a mere conduit between the worlds. I would much rather focus on you."

"Alright then," I murmur. "Can I call you Ash?"

Laughter vibrates in his chest, making the water rumble. Thick bubbles rise from its surface and burst to reveal pops of spicy menthol.

I bite down on my bottom lip, wondering if I should have chosen something less tree-like, but he pulls me into a tight hug.

"Forgive me, Sweet Human," he says between chuckles. "I am honored to receive such a name."

"If you want, I can choose something else," I say.

"Ash is perfect." He pulls back, his amber eyes twinkling. "What shall I call you?"

"My name is Emily," I reply with a smile, "But everyone calls me Milly."

"Milly," he says as though tasting the words. "I am delighted to make your acquaintance."

I suppress a smile at his understatement. He's pleasured me to an inch of my life, plundered my holes, and filled me with nearly a gallon of his release. I would say that's more than just a passing association.

He picks up a pair of wrinkled fruit the size of cherry tomatoes and rubs them between his hands. Moments later he produces a thick, white lather and works it into my wet hair.

"What's that?"

"Soapberries," he says and massages my scalp.

My eyelids flutter shut, and I relax into his gentle touch, not quite believing that this is the creature who once wanted me dead.

"That feels so good," I murmur.

"It's my pleasure," Ash replies, his voice seductive and deep. "After all, you have made me feel things beyond a tree's imagination."

After washing my hair, his fingers travel down my neck and over my shoulders. His touches are so gentle and unhurried that my heart flutters with a sense of acceptance.

"What were you doing alone in the forest last

night?" he asks.

"Running away from my life," I murmur.

He pulls me into a hug, seeming to know exactly what I need. "Tell me about it."

I'm so relaxed and off guard that I spill the entire story, starting from how I went on Tinder to meet men and ending with the showdown between me and the pack of wolves. Throughout this, Ash remains quiet, his fingers slowing.

"What's wrong?" I ask.

"Why did you marry that man?"

"Umm... Because I wanted love and a family."

"Offspring?" he asks.

"That's right. What's wrong."

"Those people are parasites who had no intention of offering you either."

"True."

"Like me."

My head snaps up. "What?"

"I wanted to feed from your blood, much like they wanted to feed from your milk. You are the most fascinating person I have ever encountered yet I was only concerned about using you for sustenance."

A breath catches in the back of my throat. The fact that he sees something in me that everyone has overlooked proves to me he's nothing like Erik and his shitty family.

Ash was upfront with me from the beginning, but with Erik, I fell in love with a carefully crafted facade. Ash is uncovering layers neither of us knew existed. He's slowly developing his humanity, but Erik was always a monster.

Even though I'm technically Ash's prisoner, I can reason with him, he listens, and he's evolving. Knowing that someone finally sees me makes up for our rocky beginning. There's no comparison with Erik.

"You're wrong." I pull back, my gaze meeting his and shake my head for emphasis.

Ash dips his neck, unable to meet my eyes, but I place a hand on his cheek.

"Have you forgotten that you saved me from a pack of wolves?" I ask.

"Because you were my prey."

"Did you ever pretend to be something you weren't?"

"No."

"From the moment you pulled me up, you let me know your intentions. Erik and his family pretended to welcome me into their fold. I didn't discover what they were doing until the last minute and when I wanted to escape, they threatened me with death."

Ash remains silent as though he still can't see the difference between his conduct and theirs.

I exhale a frustrated breath. "You showed me mercy. You could have skewered me through the chest but you took up my offer of period blood."

"Only because you had such intriguing stories," he mutters.

"At least you show an interest in what I say." I lean against his broad chest. "When you listen to me, I feel like something more than the girl who works in a bakery. You pay attention. You care. And you give me more pleasure than I could handle."

He hesitates. "You enjoy yourself that much?"

My lips curl into a smile. He knows how much I loved being fucked to within an inch of my sanity, but I think he needs to hear the words.

"Yes," I murmur. "You gave me more pleasure than any man could offer. You introduced me to things beyond my wildest fantasies. I have never climaxed harder or felt so much care."

"But I cannot give you children."

"That's not our arrangement," I reply. "The way I see myself through your eyes is a huge gift."

"Truly?" he asks, his voice filling with wonder.

"No exaggeration. My husband is the type of man who only listens to find an opening to speak. Even my friends at home loved talking more than they listened. You're different." I sigh. "Sometimes, the way you look at me makes me feel seen."

"I do not understand."

"You see things in me others don't. No one ever said I had a nice voice or ever complimented me on anything I had to say. You show me, through your words and the way you look and listen, that I'm valued."

His chest makes a deep rumble.

"I went through my whole life not being appreciated as a person. It's something I never noticed until you gave me your undivided attention."

My mind drifts through a kaleidoscope of experiences: a mother and father so consumed by their love of drugs that they had little left over for me, foster parents who treated me like a burden and a business, teachers who ignored me for their favorites, and boyfriends who only cared for sex.

I couldn't even escape being overlooked in the bakery. My colleagues were nice, but they never let me get a word in edgeways. I was always the one who smiled and listened, while they showed little interest in my life.

Then there was Erik, who only paid enough attention to get me ensnared. He and his family didn't love me. They loved what I could do for Mikael.

Drawing back, I meet his gaze, my fingers tracing

the angular planes of his face. "You taught me that I matter."

Ash exhales a long breath. "Maybe you're right."

"About what?"

"It would be wrong to keep you here against your will, but I am selfish."

"That's okay." I place a palm on his chest.

There's no heartbeat, only a gentle thrum of liquid surging beneath the surface. I can't tell if this is some form of magic or plant-based circulation, but the effect is awe-inspiring.

Ash continues working lather into my skin with touches so gentle that my eyes flutter shut. I have never felt so content.

"I don't want to let you go," he says.

There's a part of me that doesn't want to leave, but how long will I survive on berries, roots, and tree sap?

With a sigh, Ash lifts me out of the water and carries me across the cavern to a four-poster bed with curtains of white, hanging moss. They draw apart, letting him lay me down on a green mattress.

He joins me onto the thick pile of moss and pulls me into his broad chest. By now, moonlight shines through the clouds from the opening up above, casting gentle illumination.

"I want to keep you at my side until the end of

time," he murmurs into my hair, his fingers soaking up the moisture from each strand.

My heart flutters and I ignore the sensation. Being with Ash is like the best possible dream filled with pleasure and passion and wonder, but like all dreams, they must end. I keep my eyes shut partially needing to avoid responding but mostly because all that sex has left me exhausted.

He rubs soothing circles on my back, lulling me into a deep state of tranquility. No one has touched me with such tenderness since before I went into foster care.

Tears prick the backs of my eyes as my mind drifts back to the day a social worker informed me that my parents had died from overdoses.

It was the moment I realized nobody in the world would ever think of me as special... until possibly now.

"Forgive me, Milly, but I can't muster up the good conscience to set you free."

My body relaxes and my mind pulls me into slumber, safe in the hope that he'll soon develop more of a conscience.

Because if he doesn't, I will be his prisoner for what's left of my life.

Chapter Thirteen

The next few days pass in a flurry of sex, with Ash eager to find different ways of giving me pleasure and me too aroused to turn down his advances.

We spend hours talking, mostly about what it was like thousands of years ago before the Norse gods destroyed each other and the people forsook them for modern civilization.

I learn stories of Odin, Thor, and Loki, and the creatures who inhabited the nine worlds. Now that I'm no longer spinning bullshit to keep myself alive, I tell him the truth about airplanes and the tiny group of humans who may or may not have traveled to the moon.

One night, we watch the starlit sky at the highest pinnacle of the tree on a loveseat made of branches and moss. A warm breeze meanders through the leaves, carrying the scent of the forest.

A lone eagle cries out in the distance, seeming to call out for its mate.

"You must have been so lonely when everyone left," I murmur.

He takes my hand and traces his rough fingertips across my knuckles. I gaze up into his handsome features, meeting shining amber irises. He looks almost human in the soft light, save for the hairless face, but the effect is breathtakingly beautiful.

"Ragnarök may have been the end of the gods, but it destroyed me too," he murmurs. "I lay in splinters for centuries, with just a few seeds buried deep within the earth."

"How did you come back to life?" I ask.

"This forest was the scene of a battle where hundreds of warriors fell. My seeds germinated with the offering of their blood, and their flesh rotted into the ground to provide nutrients."

I lean into his side. "Is that why you need to eat people?"

"Correct," he says. "This time I have spent with you is the longest I have stayed awake. Taking your blood is a new beginning."

He reaches out, his calloused fingers ghosting along my jawline. Tingles skitter across my skin and race toward my heart. My breath catches as he leans closer, his breath warming my flesh. I straighten in the love seat, my pulse quickening in anticipation of his kiss.

His lips are softer than his hands, without a trace of woodgrain. I can't tell if that's because he deliberately made them smooth or if he's becoming more human.

I moan into the kiss, and his tongue slides into my mouth, bringing with it the gentle taste of maple syrup. Ash pulls me onto his lap, and I place both hands on his chest, desperate to feel the pounding of his heart. His skin is now butter soft, almost like suede. Power thrums beneath my palms, reminding me once more that he's a creature made of magic and wood.

"You make me feel so alive," he whispers against my lips. "I have never felt this kind of joy."

My heart swells, and I kiss back, my body melting into the warmth of his embrace. Somewhere in the back of my mind, I know I have to leave but the thought is too painful. No one has every listened to me so intently. No one has ever shown me so much appreciation. No one else has given me this level of happiness and pleasure. The connection we've created is profound.

The kiss deepens until we're so entwined that the

only thing stopping me from losing myself completely is the throbbing of my pussy.

"Ash," I groan. "Please."

"Tell me what you need," he growls.

"There's something I've always wanted to try."

He draws back, his eyes glowing like burning coals. "Name it."

Heat flares across my cheeks. I can't believe the thought tumbled through my mind but now that it's there, I can't suppress it.

"Can you adjust your body to create different shapes?"

His brows pinch together. "Am I not to your satisfaction?"

"It's not that," I say, my hands rising to his face. "You're perfect."

"Then why do you ask?"

"There's a famous story about a creature made of wood, whose nose used to expand whenever he told a lie."

Ash cocks his head to the side, his lips turning down. "But everything I have told you has been the truth."

"I know... I know." My tongue darts out to lick my lips. Shit. I'm not saying this properly. "Can you make your nose longer?"

His eyelids lower, and the tip of his nose lengthens an extra inch. "Like this?"

I clear my throat. "Make it the size of your cock."

Ash pauses, his gaze searing mine. "You wish to fuck my face?"

"Yes," I say with a groan. "I would love that."

"Then allow me to indulge your wishes." He rises off the mossy sofa, taking me with him. "May I take out your plug?"

I stare down at the tiny branch connecting our bodies. "Of course."

As he removes the tampon and absorbs it into his belly, the loveseat in the branches lengthens to form a broad platform with a near-panoramic view of the forest. Smoke rises in the distance from what I presume is Erik's farmhouse, but I turn my head in the other direction.

Ash lies on his back with his arms splayed out to the sides. His cock stands to full mast with a heavy bead of precum that's colored silver in the light of the moon.

"Is this how you want me?" he asks, his voice seductive and deep.

"That's right." I lower myself onto my hands and knees. "Now, extend your nose a little more."

His nose lengthens another few inches and forms a tiny slit. I swallow back a moan. The truth is that I never wanted to fuck Pinocchio himself, I just wish it was easier to spot a man's deception.

Some guys are such great liars that it would be helpful if there was a surefire way to see their bullshit. Other times, I just wish their noses would grow so there's something to keep me full while I'm sitting on their faces.

I hover over Ash's head, making sure to face his cock. That way, I can also keep my mouth occupied while riding his nose.

Ash's hot breath warms my folds, making my clit swell.

"You look so enchanting like this with your cunt closing in on my face," he growls, his words vibrating against my flesh.

"Oh fuck," I reply. "I mean... thanks."

He holds me steady by the hips, not forcing or guiding my movements like most men would, but providing support and easing the pressure off my thighs.

The tip of his nose brushes against my wet folds, making me shiver. A thick droplet of fluid falls from my pussy, and he moans.

I lower myself onto his nose. It's tapered at the tip and flares gently at the nostrils. Even though it's nowhere as huge as his cock, I still feel a delicious stretch. Woodgrain massages my inner walls with back-and-forth motions as though the flesh that makes up his nose is sentient.

"Is that alright?" he asks.

"Fuck, yeah," I groan and lean forward to support my weight on my hands and knees. "Now lick my clit."

He swipes his tongue across my engorged clit, his movements languid and leisurely. Pleasure ripples through my core, drawing out a gasp. My muscles tighten around his nose as he continues to lick and suck and infuse my body with delicious sensations.

I ride his nose, my hips rocking back and forth to maximize the friction. Ash's regular cock sways with the force of my movements, as though begging for attention.

Once I build up a steady rhythm, I reach out and wrap my fingers around his shaft.

Ash's deep groan reverberates against my folds, adding to the pleasure.

"That's it," I cry out. "Don't stop."

He licks faster, his tongue lashing my clit with firm strokes.

I lower my mouth to his cockhead, meeting him suck for suck, lick for lick, my hands stroking his pulsing shaft. It's so hot and thrumming and realistic that I almost forget he's an ancient tree.

Pressure gathers in my core, spurred on by the

tongue swirling around my clit. It builds and builds until I reach the point of no return. My walls close in around his nose as a powerful orgasm burns through my insides like wildfire. I scream so loud that flocks of birds burst out of the trees and into the skies.

Ash roars, the sound vibrating through my pussy, and his cock erupts with warm fluid. I open my mouth, eager to coat my tongue with his syrupy cum.

I massage his shaft through the spurts, while his tongue flickers and flutters against my clit, triggering a second orgasm. Ash groans, and his nose releases a burst of liquid that splashes against my walls.

As the orgasm subsides, I collapse against him, exhausted and satisfied.

"That was amazing," I say through panting breaths.

"It was," Ash replies, his voice a monotone.

"What's wrong?"

He pulls me off his face and settles me onto his side. "I don't ever want to let you go."

Chapter Fourteen

After reinserting the wooden tampon, Ash gathers me in his arms, and a branch transports us back into the tree's cavern. The space now has a permanent four-poster bed, a water fountain, a sofa, and an open-plan bathroom.

He settles me under a huge sunflower that drenches us both with hot water.

"You've turned this place into a home," I murmur.

"I want you to be comfortable," he replies.

"You know I can't stay."

Ash rubs some soapberries between his hands and glides his foamy palms over my body. His touch is gentle, almost reverent, as though he's committing the contours of my body to memory.

Steam rises from the water, but the air is thick

with tension of what's left unsaid. There's enough humanity in Ash to understand why he can't keep me here forever, but he isn't ready to admit that to himself.

I lower my head, allowing him to massage the tight muscles of my neck. We both know why they've gone rigid but neither of us wants to rehash the discussion of why he can't keep me as his captive.

The water cuts off, and he wraps his arms around my body and soaks the water from my skin, leaving me fresh and clean and dry.

We walk hand in hand to the bed and collapse onto the mattress, our bodies entangling. Ash lays me on my back and trails kisses over my face until my heart flutters, and I melt into his touches.

"I know I can't keep you," he murmurs. "But letting go of you will be worse than Ragnarok."

"Ash, I'm sorry—"

"Don't speak. Just sleep in my arms."

A sigh escapes my nostrils. "I don't want to be separated from you, but is there a way to leave the tree?"

He pulls back, his features a mask of confusion. "I am the tree."

"I know, but..." My words fizzle into nothing as I puzzle out how to solve this problem. "Can you at least leave the trunk?"

Ash pauses. "I haven't tried."

"Why not?"

"This is the first time I've created an extension of myself."

"Oh."

"Milly?" he asks.

"What?"

"Rest. We will speak more on this tomorrow."

The next morning, I wake up alone. There's no sign of movement in the cavern, which is even more unusual because Ash never leaves my side.

I sit up, swing my legs off the mattress, and part the lichen curtains. "Ash?"

No answer.

When I step out of the bed, all the furniture is gone.

A warm breeze blows in from behind, making me turn around to find that one of the windows has expanded to form a door.

Is this a test?

"Ash?" I say a little louder. "Where are you?"

"Always here," he replies.

I turn in a circle, my gaze sweeping across the empty walls. "Where? I can't see you."

"You are looking at me."

"Is this some sort of joke? Come out."

"I am the tree."

A huff leaves my chest. "This is about what I said last night. I know you're the tree, but I want to see the wooden man—"

"Simulacrum—"

"Okay, the simulacrum. Where is it?"

A huge sigh fills the cavern with oxygen. "Milly, you are no longer bleeding."

I glance down between my legs to find the branch gone. "So, what?"

"I promised myself that I would keep you until the blood runs dry."

Tears prick the backs of my eyes. Was he using me all this time for my period blood? He's already glutted himself on Olivia and William. I was just dessert. Now that I'm no longer bleeding, he thinks I'm surplus to requirements?

I struggle to say the words because it's hard enough to be trapped and manipulated by one lover for my body fluids, only for another to do the same. But isn't this what I wanted? In theory, yes. In practice, I can't believe he would let me go without a fight.

"Is that all I meant to you?" I whisper. "A delicacy?"

"Never," he says.

"Why are you casting me out?"

"Because you're human," he growls. "You cannot live on love and sunlight. You need people, you need experiences, you need purpose. I can't give you anything but this cage."

"Why don't you say that to my face?"

Ash huffs a laugh. There's no mirth in the sound, only bitterness. "One more touch of your skin, and you would remain my prisoner until the end of time."

"You don't mean that," I whisper.

"Leave," he says. "I have pieced together some fabrics and a strong pair of boots. My offshoots will guide your passage to another part of the woods, where you can catch transportation back to England."

I swallow hard, my heart aching so terribly that it spreads to the back of my throat.

He's setting me free.

This is what I wanted. This is what I hoped for. This is what we argued about every day. Why am I so desperate to stay?

Because over these few days, Ash has given me more care, compassion, and connection than I've had in my entire life. He's the only person who has changed to accommodate me.

"I don't want to go," I say, my voice barely a whisper.

No reply.

"Ash, please." Tears spill down my cheeks and onto my breasts. "Aren't you at least going to come out and say goodbye?"

"Milly," he growls, sounding exactly as he did the night he captured me in his branches. "Leave now, or I will close all openings and you will never know freedom."

Alarm flares in my chest. I run to the table, gather up the pile of clothing and boots, and rush out through the door. The panic is futile, considering that Ash's branches stretch across the vast clearing, but the thought of being trapped is equally as terrifying as losing Ash.

I turn around for one last look at the cavity that was my home for a week, but all I find is a tiny knot within a vast tree trunk.

He's shut me out.

"Ash?"

The ground rumbles, and roots rise from the grass and nudge my feet toward the edge of the clearing. I continue away from his trunk, my heart dragging along the forest floor, all the while feeling the weight of his gaze on my back.

I keep walking until I reach the edge of the clearing, where spindly seedlings wilt under the weight of Ash's presence.

Turning back, I search Ash's trunk for signs of the being who helped me get over my husband's betrayal, only to find an unmoving tree.

"Goodbye, Ash," I whisper into the breeze.

He doesn't reply but when I turn back, a path opens up in the saplings, presumably leading me out of the forest.

I unfold the pile of clothes, only to find the same kind of leathery pouch Ash used to deliver my meals. The sight of it makes my throat tighten. How long did he spend preparing for my departure?

The clothes are made from rough squares of fabric stitched together to form a long dress with a hooded robe. After putting them on, I slip into the boots.

With a heavy sigh, I set off down the path, not looking back. Tears stream freely down my face. I don't remember feeling this kind of sorrow when I escaped Erik, only fear and anger and disgust. Leaving Ash is like tearing out my heart.

Along the way, creatures eye me from a distance. I spot foxes, moose, and wild boars, but no sign of wolves. None of them approach, not even something as small as a rabbit.

By the time the path leads me to a road on the

edge of the forest, the sun dips low in the horizon, casting long shadows. I turn around, desperate for a final look at Ash, only for my view to be obscured by the trees.

"Ash?" I say.

He doesn't answer. I'm too far out of his orbit.

An hour later, I walk along the roadside. It's a two-lane highway with fluorescent markers illuminated only by moonlight.

Ash has probably gone to sleep for a century now, or maybe two, since he ate both William and Olivia. I don't have time to consider it because I hear the rumble of an approaching vehicle.

My heart skips, and I retreat into the trees, just in case it's Mikael or Erik. Their farm extends over a hundred hectares and it's not like they have neighbors.

An exhaust pipe sputters, suggesting that whoever is driving can't afford the maintenance. Hope soars in my chest, and my feet carry me back to the edge of the road. Nobody in the Freyman family would drive an old banger that pollutes the air with smoke.

I wave my arms, and the car slows to a stop. The driver is a thin figure who leans across the passenger seat to wind down the window.

Before he has the chance to speak, I ask in broken Swedish, “Do you speak English?”

“Of course,” he replies, his accent thick. “How may I help you?”

“Are you going to town?” I ask.

He nods.

“My car broke down a few kilometers back.” I wave my arm in a vague direction. “Could I please have a ride?”

The stranger gives me a warm smile. “My son is a mechanic. You can stay in his waiting room while he picks up your vehicle.”

“Thanks,” I murmur, my insides curdling at the lie.

Slipping inside, I shut the door, then the central locking activates with a click. I turn to ask him what he’s doing, just as his fist lands on the side of my face, knocking me unconscious.

Chapter Fifteen

A large hand slaps me across the face, and I wake up with a gasp. My eyes snap open and I stared into the cold glare of Erik's grandmother. Clara hovers over me, her features twisted with hate.

My head pounds, mostly because of that knockout punch. It's been years since someone hit me so hard, and my eye is already swollen. I try to rise, but my shoulders are strapped to a bed. There's a tenderness to my breasts that feels worse than any kind of PMS, and my nipples feel raw. I dart my gaze from side to side, only to find I'm in some kind of infirmary.

Clara steps backward with her arms folded over her chest. "We went to a lot of trouble to find you. All our employees are scouring the forest. Poor

Olivia and William haven't yet returned to the farmhouse."

My jaw clenches.

That's because they're dead.

I'm already in more trouble than I can handle. No need to make matters worse.

"Why are you keeping me?" I ask.

"When you married into this family, you agreed to feed Mikael," she says through clenched teeth. "We won't let you run around trying to collect alimony like a gold digger."

"There was a gun pointing at me the entire time. They threatened to kill me if I refused."

Clara sniffs. "A girl like you should feel lucky to be offered a life of luxury. If you continue to be difficult, we'll have to make other arrangements."

The implication of her words makes my spine shiver. I don't need to be a mind reader to know she's talking about my death.

Since my plan to hitchhike into town has failed, and I have no chance of escaping, I'll have to play along with these bastards until I get an opening.

"What's going to happen, now?" I ask.

"We've kept you on a diet of protein-rich fluid to improve your breast milk, along with a concentrated formula of lactation herbs."

My lips tighten, and I realize that some of the

discomfort I felt on the side of my face is coming from a feeding tube. I turn my gaze to a thin, plastic pipe leading to a transparent bag held up by an intravenous pole.

"Bloody hell," I whisper.

This is heinous.

Sweat breaks out across my skin, and my breath turns shallow as I process the reality of my predicament. I'm no stranger to criminals. My time in the British care system has exposed me to juvenile delinquents, and the bakery has been held up a few times at gunpoint.

These people are something else entirely. This is a whole new level of depravity.

I'm in way over my head.

A knock sounds on the door, and Erik steps in, his blue eyes arctic.

"You embarrassed me at the wedding," he says, his voice as cold as his glare.

I bow my head, clench my jaw, and curl my hands into fists. The man in the car already punched me unconscious, and Clara slapped my face. I'm not in the mood for any more pain.

He advances on me and grabs my chin. "What do you have to say for yourself?"

"How long have I been here?" I ask.

His brow furrows. "What?"

"You two could have made me drink the herbs, but you didn't." I glare at him out of the corner of my eye. "How long have I been unconscious?"

He chuckles. "See, Grandma? This one is intelligent."

She huffs. "You should have chosen someone more obedient. This one is troublesome."

"How are the herbs coming along?" Erik asks as though I'm not in the room.

"See for yourself." Clara bustles out of the room and closes the door with a click.

Erik advances on me, his eyes on my breasts. My heart spikes as he swipes his tongue over his lips, and I thrash within my bindings.

"You've increased two cup sizes," he says, his voice breathy.

That explains the tender breasts.

"Stay away from me." I kick out to the side, but there's a leather strap around my ankles.

"You're my wife," he snarls.

"Only under duress," I snap back. "Or have you forgotten about the gun?"

He sits on the edge of my bed and reaches for my chest. I'm wearing a white gown with buttons running down the front, and he yanks it open, sending the fastenings flying across the bedspread.

"A week," he says.

"What?" I ask, my voice rising several octaves.

"In answer to your question of how long you've been here."

Shit.

"Erik, don't do this," I whisper.

"You swore to love and honor and obey."

"It doesn't count if your grandfather's pointing a gun into my ribs."

He reaches into my gown and eases out my breast. It's warmer than usual and more tender, which I suppose is due to the intravenous herbs.

"Stop it," I yell, my voice shrill.

"Your milk will come in any moment now," he murmurs, his eyes on my nipple. "And I'm going to be the first to have a taste."

I jerk to the side, trying to throw myself off the mattress, but it's no use. They've strapped me so securely to the bed that I'm helpless.

"Why?" I rasp.

"Why did I choose you?" he asks. "Because you have phenomenal tits."

"Why are you doing this?"

"We have a condition in our family that's passed through the Y chromosome." He brushes a strand of hair off my face. "Until we found the cure, none of our ancestors lived past fifty."

I release a panicked laugh. "Your remedy is breast

milk?"

"Human milk infused with a blend of specific herbs." His fingers trail down my neck, making my skin ripple with revulsion.

This sounds like bullshit, but makes a twisted form of sense. If herbs can trigger lactation and substances can pass through breast milk to harm a baby, maybe the opposite is true.

"Have you tried mixing your herbs with formula?" I ask.

"No." He slips his fingers down to my collarbone.

"Come near me, and I'll scream murder."

He slides his palm down my enlarged breast and closes his fingers around my nipple. Back when we were dating, something like that would have gotten me excited. Now, his touch feels like fire.

"You know how much I like it when you're noisy." He parts his lips and lowers his mouth to my breast.

I scream so loud into his ear that he jerks back with a scowl.

His nostrils flare. "What are you doing?"

"Saying no." I kick out at him, missing his crotch by several inches. "If you want breast milk, go to your mother."

Oh, wait. She's dead.

I say that part in my mind since I still have some level of self-preservation.

Erik bares his teeth and lunges at me, only for the door to slam open.

"Get away from the girl," Mikael says, his voice harsh. "The combination of herbs we fed her is not good for you."

"She's my wife." Erik straightens and steps back from the bed.

"Evidently, she's no longer interested." Mikael's voice is even colder than his grandson's. "This mess is entirely your fault, Erik. You should have at least given her an indication of what was expected as a wife in this family, yet your failure led to a shotgun wedding. If she continues to be so miserable, her milk will sour."

My jaw drops, and I glance from grandfather to son. The comment about sour milk rolls off me like a breeze. I can't help but notice that Erik is in his prime, yet he cowers in the presence of the old man.

"The time was never right to explain," Erik mutters.

Mikael's lip curls. "Get out."

Erik shoots me a vengeful glare before walking out of the room with his head bowed. He doesn't even slam the door.

My mind makes rapid-fire connections. Mikael is

the true power in the family, even though he walks with a stick and has nine toes in the grave. If I'm going to get any measure of freedom it's going to be through him. Mikael makes the decisions, yet he's the one I'm most likely to defeat in a fight.

He ambles across the room and lowers himself into the bedside chair with a groan. "I apologize for my grandson's conduct. He was supposed to make you so deeply in love that you would do anything to help our family."

I would laugh at the ridiculousness of that statement. First of all, no amount of sweet talk could ever get me to agree to this atrocity. Secondly, the decade I spent in foster care taught me to get used to disappointment. I wait for him to apologize for his own shitty actions, but he only offers me a rheumy smile.

"You have to understand, Milly, that I'm not an unreasonable man."

"Are you sure about that?" I ask, my voice trembling.

"Your escape into the woods set back our schedule by a week. Erik is already back on the dating websites, searching for your replacement, and I'm not getting any younger."

His gaze sweeps down to my exposed breast, and all the fine hairs on the back of my neck stand on end.

"How long does it usually take for the milk to come?" I rasp.

He leans toward me at a snail's pace, his wrinkled lips parting. "Two or three weeks, depending on the method used to stimulate lactation."

"You mean the herbs?"

"Clara believes manual pumps are the way to get you to produce faster, and Erik agrees." Mikael shakes his head, still advancing on me at the speed of a tortoise. "The only way to get you to produce faster is from mouth to nipple."

Fuck.

"Wait a minute," I say, my voice trembling. "You're going to suck me?"

"How else can a man obtain his milk?"

A bottle, a carton, in his cappuccino. Anything but from me. I want to scream all these things but it would be pointless.

I swallow hard, my mind whirring for an escape. Mikael doesn't give a shit that I refuse to be a part of his freaky family, let alone feed him my breast milk.

Appealing to his better nature won't work because he's rotten, but what if I convinced him to change location? What if I demanded a romantic setting, such as underneath an ancient tree?

"Breastfeeding is a sacred act between a mother and child," I say.

"I will allow you to call me baby," he says, his tongue sliding over his lips and leaving a glistening trail of moisture.

"And it shouldn't be done while I'm strapped to a bed."

"Agreed."

He's so close that my skin tightens into goosebumps.

"There's a beautiful spot I know in the woods. We can have a picnic and relax. I'll even let you rest your head on my thighs while you feed."

"Sounds delightful," he murmurs, his tepid breath fanning my nipple.

Fuck, shit, and damn him to hell.

This man is relentless.

Time to change tactics.

What I'm about to say next is risky and will either get me into worse trouble or set me free. Judging by what Mikael intends to do to me, I've run out of options.

I shrink away from his mouth. "But there's something I want from you."

His gaze rises to meet mine. "Birkin bags? Kelly Bags? Whatever you want, name it."

"Since you're planning on sucking my nipple, I want to suck your cock."

Chapter Sixteen

Mikael's face goes slack. He draws back, finally giving me space to breathe.

"What did you say?"

I sit straighter within my restraints. "You're planning on forcibly taking my breastmilk."

He nods. "Correct."

"In exchange, I want your cum."

He darts his gaze to the door. "Do you know what you're saying?"

"That I want to wrap my lips around your cock and suck it until you spurt? That I want to drain your balls of all your spunk? And when you can't take it anymore, I'll oil up my hand and pump you until you sputter?"

His breath turns shallow, and his Adam's apple bobs up and down. "You would do this to me?"

"Why not?" I say, my brows rising. "It's only fair, considering what you plan on doing to me."

Mikael turns his head toward the door again and pauses for several moments, seeming to listen out for his wife.

I resist the urge to roll my eyes. Men are so fucking simple. The moment a woman throws sex into the conversation, they're derailed until after they cum.

He turns back to me, his eyes shining with unusual clarity. "Very well. I accept your bargain."

My eyes flutter shut and I exhale the longest breath of relief. "I can't wait."

"Then you had better get started." Mikael rises off the bed and fumbles at his fly. "From this moment, I will call you Milky and you must call me Pappy."

I clench my jaw. This is exactly what I feared. Not the shitty nicknames but the prospect of him skipping ahead and demanding a blowjob.

"Have you taken your Viagra?" I ask.

He rears back. "What?

"Or erection herbs," I say, my head flicking toward the intravenous feeding bag. "If I have to take something so I can produce milk, so do you. I won't be satisfied with just one squirt."

Mikael gives me a solemn nod. "I will be back as soon as I can."

"Don't forget about the romantic location, Pappy," I add.

Before he can answer, the door swings open with a bang. Clara steps in, her shoulders tensing. How much of our conversation did she overhear? Nothing about this woman says she'll take kindly to me propositioning her husband.

"Erik says the girl is giving him trouble," she says, her features an unreadable mask.

I freeze in place, my heart plummeting to my stomach.

"He was trying to force the girl against her will," Mikael says. "I walked in just in time to stop the boy."

Clara's gaze travels from me to the old man, her eyes narrowing at the corners. The entire situation makes me want to scream.

Why can't she give Mikael her milk? Why can't they set up the old bastard with his own feeding tube? Why do they have to capture unwilling young women when there's formula, milk banks, or consenting women with lactation kinks?

I'm so sick of these people and their coercive bullshit that I'm ready to vomit.

"Leave us," she says.

Mikael turns to me, his eyes twinkling. "We will resume our conversation later."

"Thanks for the discussion about the herbs," I say.

He walks out, passing his wife without a second glance. As soon as the door clicks shut, she advances on me with her fists clenched.

"What are you planning?" she snarls.

"Nothing," I say with a yawn. "But I'm curious about why you're putting another woman in this situation. Did you have to breastfeed Mikael's grandfather, too?"

"I did my duty." She bustles over to a metal trolley and picks up a plunger-looking device attached to a little bottle. "As will you."

A shudder runs down my spine. "Is that—"

"This pump will stimulate your lactation." She attaches one to my exposed breast.

I shudder as the contraption creates a vacuum that tugs and releases my nipple. It's painful at first and then simply uncomfortable.

"Is this how I'll feed Mikael?" I ask.

"If I have anything to do with it," she mutters. "When I was in your position, his grandfather wanted me to stroke his penis as he fed."

"So, you're protecting me from a pervert?"

"Making sure you don't steal my husband," she snaps. "Little bitches like you like to marry older men for their money."

"If you're so worried about me, then pay a professional."

"If only it were that simple," she mutters.

"What do you mean?"

"Women in love produce oxytocin, which gets passed on in the breast milk. When you fell hopelessly in love with my grandson, he was supposed to coax you into feeding my husband."

"Okay, then cast me out and let him charm someone else."

"No time. Mikael is fading fast."

"Then give him your milk." I should stop talking and continue refining my plans. Nothing I say to Clara will work, since she doesn't give a damn, but I need to try, at least out of morbid curiosity.

She flashes her teeth. "Do you think I'm stupid?"

I flinch. Is she a mind reader? "No."

"Each man requires a different combination of herbs to activate the milk's healing powers. Mine is attuned to Mikael's grandfather's." I'm about to ask how she can feed her son, but she continues. "Because I carried William, the herbal combination in my blood became attuned to him."

My eyes squeeze shut, and despair washes

through my veins like acid. They're not just sickos. They really need me for survival.

"But I don't love Erik," I whisper.

"Nonsense," she snaps. "You're already in love with our luxury and wealth. This is a thousand times better than living in a dingy room in a polluted city and baking cakes that taste like shit."

Fuck. I crack open an eye to glare into her spiteful face. Did she have to add insult to my incarceration?

"I'd rather live in the gutter and eat shit than go anywhere near your man."

She curls her lip. "Keep it that way. If I catch you making a move on my Mikael, I'll put a bullet through your head."

"If you were that worried about your husband, you wouldn't be forcing me to lactate."

Ignoring me, Clara turns to the mechanism attached to the breast pumps and turns the dial. The uncomfortable sucking sensation intensifies, making me wince.

What a bitch.

The next few days are agonizing, and not just because my breasts are on fire. Each day, I dread the return of Mikael, but Clara's constant presence is enough to keep him away. More importantly, my heart aches for Ash. I miss the tranquility of his cavern, the touch of his soft leather skin, and his constant presence at my side. I miss his stories about the time of the gods and the wonder he found in the most basic of technology.

My eyes sting every time I look out of the window into the distant forest, knowing he's probably fallen asleep for another century. It's how he copes with having lost everything.

I'm beginning to know how that feels.

Erik drops in occasionally to update me with the progress of the search for his next wife. He looks stressed, as does everyone else since William and Olivia still haven't returned from the forest.

Eventually, my breasts produce milk. Clara removes the feeding tube and takes away a sample to test its quality. I send a silent prayer to anyone listening that it's full of stress hormones or something equally as harmful.

Later that evening, the door swings open, and Mikael creeps into the room.

"Your sample is healthy," he says, his tongue sliding out of his lips.

My hackles rise and my heart pounds so hard

that my ribs rattle. I squirm within my restraints, already knowing that there isn't a thing I can do to stop him from sucking my breasts against my will.

"Have you considered what I asked?" I rasp.

He glances over his shoulder. "Clara is watching her soap opera. We have plenty of time."

"Not here," I whisper.

He nods, his gaze roaming my body.

My skin crawls, and I try not to flinch as he unbuckles my restraints. Every fiber of my being wants to knock the old man down and escape into the forest, but he's stronger than he looks. There's also a twinkle in his eyes that suggests he might have already gotten a little vitality from my sample of milk.

A man steps into the room as the last restraint falls to the side. It's the bastard in the old banger who punched me in the face.

"Who's that?" I ask.

"Peter is a member of the search party I sent after William and Olivia," Mikael says. "I believe you're already acquainted."

Peter gives me a blank stare.

Shit. I might have been able to fight one old man but not two.

"Can I at least choose the location for our picnic under the stars?" I rasp.

Mikael smiles, exposing long teeth and eyes so bright that I feel like I'm staring into the face of the devil.

"Anything you wish," he says, his voice breathy. "Peter here will keep us both safe."

Moments later, I'm wearing a man's overcoat that smells of mothballs and sitting on Mikael's lap on the back of an oversized quad bike. The forest whizzes past, but my nostrils fill with the rancid scent of decay.

He cups my breasts and grinds his erection into my ass.

"You feel that?" he growls.

"What?"

"I took four doses of our male enhancer in case you feel extra ravenous."

My jaw clenches. I glare into Peter's back, wishing Erik was here instead of him, so I could murder them both.

"What's that story your grandmother told you about the forest?" I ask.

"I don't follow." He rolls his hips, trying to nestle his erection against my slit.

Shudders run down my spine, and I resist the urge to scream. "Your great-grandfather threatened her with some kind of plant."

He chuckles, the sound low and rusty, making my hackles rise. "Don't tell me you believed it?"

"I wasn't sure," I murmur.

"It's just a legend. This piece of land has been in our family since before the time of record keeping. Whenever a person goes missing in the forest, people blame the tree." He pats my thigh. "Are we heading in the right direction?"

The trees thin the way they did the night I ran, and my heart skips. Coming here is a huge gamble. If Ash has fallen asleep, then Mikael will live long enough to expect a blow job.

Shudders run down my spine. Sometimes, I don't think through the consequences of my actions and I end up in a fuck-ton of trouble.

I should have known something was up when I caught the attention of a ridiculously handsome man on a dating site. I should have poked at the whirlwind romance and not allowed myself to get swept away into a flurry of gifts, fancy dinners, and sweet words.

Mikael nuzzles my neck. "What are you thinking about?"

"Romance," I mutter.

His deep chuckle makes the fine hairs on the back of my neck stand on end. "My heart belongs to Clara, but you can have my cum."

My stomach lurches. I bite back a scream and remain silent, my mind scrambling for a plan B in case I can't awaken Ash. Fighting a frail old man is no longer an option because he's brought a healthy protector capable of knocking me out with a single punch.

Peter stops at the clearing, dismounts, and offers me a gloved hand.

I rear back, my gaze dropping to his gun holster.

Mikael squeezes me around the waist. "Take his hand. He only punched you because every employee was under orders to return you by any means necessary."

Peter's grin broadens.

The old man's erection shifts under my ass, making me gag. I take Peter's hand and let him pull me off the quad bike.

After helping Mikael out, Peter jogs to the back of the bike, extracts a huge bag, and tucks a blanket under his arm. I stare straight ahead into the clearing, where Ash stands so tall and proud that I can barely see his branches.

My pulse rattles through my skull, drowning out the sounds of the forest. Ash had better be awake.

Mikael leans into me and whispers, "You never explained how you survived in the forest without weapons. Our land has a high concentration of predators."

"I hid inside the hollow of a tree."

As he rubs circles on my lower back, I step forward out of reach and stalk toward Ash's trunk.

"Are you there?" I whisper, my voice trembling. "I know you told me to leave, but I can't stop thinking about you. I'm in trouble—"

Mikael grabs my shoulder. "Don't walk ahead."

There's a gun in his right hand, and I can't help but wonder if it's for me or for the wolves. Peter jogs ahead of us, lays down the blanket, and places a hamper in the corner. He steps back a few paces and points a rifle into the woods.

It's a miracle that I managed to stay alive the night I ran away.

"Help me onto the blanket." Mikael grabs my hand.

My heart slams itself against its cage as Peter eases the old man down. The wind blows through Ash's canopy, rustling the leaves, but the branches show no signs of life.

Mikael lies on his back. With a groan, he raises his hips and reaches for his fly.

I yank my gaze toward the tree trunk, unable to witness the horror unfolding on the blanket. Ash has to be asleep. He would have said something otherwise. With a deep breath, I ready myself to scream when a gunshot rings through the air.

"Bastard," yells a shrill voice.

Clara emerges from the woods, wearing a snowsuit and earmuffs, and holding a double-barreled shotgun.

Chapter Seventeen

By the time I whirl around to see Mikael's reaction, his fly is already open and he's palming his cock.

I skitter backward, my ears ringing from the gunshot and from her final warning.

"Peter," Mikael rasps.

Clara swings the gun in my direction. "What are you doing with my husband, you little bitch?"

I raise my palms and back toward the tree trunk. "Think about it," I say. "When you were in my position sixty years ago, did you want to touch your grandfather-in-law's cock?"

Her lips tremble, and her gaze darts from me to Mikael.

"Don't listen to her, darling," the old man says. "She propositioned me."

"Why would I when I'm married to a man my own age?" I say, meaning every word. "You accused me of wanting Mikael for his money, which is stupid. If I wait long enough, Erik will be the patriarch."

Clara breathes hard, her eyes shining with tears.

Guilt twangs my heart at the sight of her confusion, even though this woman deserves none of my pity. I'm not the type of woman who messes with other people's men but these circumstances are extraordinary. Clara is just as terrible as everyone else in this family.

"Tell your man to put down his gun," she says, her voice trembling.

"Do it," Mikael says.

"What about the bears?" Peter asks.

"Then aim the gun somewhere else."

Peter points the gun at me. I take one step backward, followed by another and another, my legs trembling. How did my plan backfire so spectacularly?

Ash was supposed to hear my distress, scoop up my enemies, and skewer their hearts. Instead, two maniacs are pointing guns at my chest while a third still can't keep his erection in his pants.

"I don't want any trouble," I rasp. "Please, don't shoot."

"You tried to seduce my husband," Clara says, her voice thick.

"Darling," Mikael says. "I could never be swayed by a low-level English slut. She kept begging to suck my cock, and I was weak."

"Why didn't you say no?" she says through sobs.

My nostrils flare. The worst part of this is that Mikael is almost telling the truth.

The old man continues his line of bullshit, recasting me as the villain, while Clara's face turns redder and redder.

"We can keep her sedated so she won't tempt me while I feed," Mikael says.

"But that will taint the milk," Clara says.

Mikael raises himself onto his elbows. "Then I will go without. Erik has a few more prospects. We can replace this whore in no time and find a more modest girl."

The old woman's breath catches. "You would let me kill her?"

"Don't listen to him," I say, my back against the tree trunk. "He'll do the same with the next girl."

"Shut up!"

Clara's gun goes off, but I'm already darting to the side. A bullet lodges in the trunk with an explosion of sap and bark. I break into a sprint, hoping to outrun Clara's insanity but she shoots again.

Heat sears through my shoulder. I stumble but manage to stay on my feet.

Clara's shrill cry echoes through the trees. I whirl around to find her suspended in midair, a branch impaling her chest.

Peter shoots. A vine snakes around his neck, jerking him into the trunk. Both guns clatter to the ground.

My heart leapfrogs to the back of my throat.

Ash is awake.

Mikael crawls toward me, his features twisted with hatred. "Is this your doing?"

I raise my chin. "You asked how I survived and I told you. In the hollow of a tree."

"Call it off." His gaze darts toward his wife.

"The way I asked you to call off the wedding?" I ask. "Where was your mercy when I was strapped to that bed and force-fed those herbs?"

He opens his mouth to respond, but I cut him off. "William and Olivia came here looking for me and they met the same fate."

His features drop. "You killed my son?"

"He made the mistake of shooting the tree," I say, my voice trembling. "If Clara hadn't turned her gun on me, she'd still be alive."

Mikael turns to the limp, hanging body of his wife and sobs. "You led us all into a trap."

"Just like your family lures innocent women with the promise of love. You have so much wealth and herbal remedies at your disposal, yet you choose to force girls to produce milk for you. This is what happens when you exploit others."

Mikael crawls across the clearing, his arms trembling. "You won't get away with murdering my wife and son."

Now that I'm no longer under the shock of being shot, the pain rises to the surface. Blood flows freely down my arm, and I shrink away from the old man.

"Get away from me if you don't want to die," I say.

"Only one person will be dying, and that's you." Mikael raises a gun.

Leaping to the side, I miss the bullet by several inches. Bark explodes at my back, and I cry out. Ash's branches swipe overhead in respond to all those attacks, but why is he still silent?

Mikael's scream echoes through the clearing. I turn to find roots rising from the ground and coiling around his body before pulling him under.

I double over and rest my forearms on my thighs. Spots appear before my eyes, and my breath comes in shallow pants. I can't get enough air into my lungs.

This has to be some kind of panic attack. Everyone is dead, but where is Ash?

Moments pass, and my pulse slows. The roaring between my ears fades to a dull hum. My skin tightens with the sensation of being watched, and I force myself upright.

So far, Ash has only protected himself—not me, and I have no idea why. In a moment, the predators will catch the scent of death and come prowling. I don't want to be there when they arrive.

I inch toward Clara's limp body and search in the dim light for her gun. Maybe I should just head for the quad bike but I can't be sure that someone or something won't attack me on the journey out of the forest.

"Ash?" I whisper, already knowing he won't reply.

After poking around in the clover, my fingers brush against metal. I pick up Clara's shotgun and turn a slow circle.

Glowing eyes watch from the shadows. I freeze, counting at least four pairs.

"Stay away," I growl.

Strong arms wrap around my waist, and I scream. The shotgun goes off in the direction of the creatures, who scatter.

"It's me." Ash's deep voice rumbles in my ear. "You're safe."

I drop the gun and whirl around in his arms, only to stare into a pair of hazel eyes with glowing flecks of amber.

"Ash?" I pull out of his hold and take him in.

Something about him is different. Standing before me is a man with long brown hair and olive skin without a trace of woodgrain. He's no longer a work of art but still retains his masculine beauty.

"Ash?"

"It's me," he says.

My hand trembles as it rises to his face. Ash takes my wrist and places it over his chest.

A strong, steady heartbeat reverberates against my palm, making me gasp.

"Are you alive?"

Chapter Eighteen

I sway on my feet with Ash's hand around my wrist the only thing keeping me upright. How on earth did he become so lifelike?

Ash gazes down at me, his eyes shimmering. They're now framed by thick lashes and dark eyebrows.

My other hand rises to his face. His cheeks are still high and prominent but covered in warm living flesh. There's a softness to his lips that didn't exist before and soft stubble on his jaw.

His brow furrows and his gaze locks onto my shoulder. "You're hurt."

I wince. "It's just a flesh wound."

"Who did this to you?" he growls.

I flick my head toward Clara, whose body swings lifelessly from a high branch.

Ash bares his teeth. "She's already dead."

"Don't you remember killing her?" I ask with a smile.

"Should have taken my time," he mutters.

He wraps a hand around my bicep and holds it steady as a branch lowers itself from above. Warm liquid trickles down from a quartet of flower heads and washes away the blood.

Another branch delivers a leathery bandage that glistens with a liquid that looks green in the moonlight.

"What are you doing?"

"This is willow bark infused with the gel of a healing succulent."

"Like aloe vera?"

His lips quirk into the tiniest of smiles. "Same family."

Ash applies the leathery bark like a bandage, and the pain subsides. I know enough about herbs from spending time with Erik and the Freyman family to understand that white willow bark contains a compound similar to aspirin. It's a popular ingredient in their medicinal blends.

He hovers his hand over my wound and cools it until the flesh goes numb, and my shoulders sag with relief.

"I'm sorry for taking so long," he murmurs.

"What happened to you?"

"When you left, I thought I could fall asleep for centuries to numb the pain of losing you, but my consciousness wouldn't allow me to rest."

My throat thickens. That's exactly how I felt on the walk out of the forest.

"I went deep into the earth to consult the Well of Wisdom to see if there was a way we could be together."

"What did it say?" I whisper.

"That we are different beings. While you are mortal, I am eternal." Ash lowers his head. "It reminded me that I would watch you one day wither and die."

"That's true."

"There was a choice. I could retain my immortality and cast off my heart, or sacrifice it to be the man you want." He gazes down at me, his eyes glistening. "I chose you."

"Are you still the tree?" I ask.

"We are now separate beings. While I can control the tree, all my consciousness now dwells in this body."

"So, you'll die like me?"

He nods. "I plan on transferring as much life-force I can to keep you strong, but I plan on dying the moment you expire."

Warmth rushes to my heart and fills it with so much joy that it spills over to my chest. The butterflies in my stomach awaken from slumber and take flight.

"You chose me," I say.

"Without hesitation," he replies with a smile of straight, white teeth. "And I am so sorry for taking so long to come to your defense."

"What happened?"

Ash's features fall, and he lowers his forehead to mine. "My consciousness was too far away to register your presence. What you saw earlier was a natural defense mechanism. I would never lie dormant when sensing you're in danger."

"I was worried for a moment," I murmur.

"Nothing will ever come between us again."

The air thickens with the weight of those words, feeling like he's made an oath to the gods. I lean against him, basking in his presence, and taking in his cedar wood scent.

"All those times you insisted on being the tree and now you gave it up for me," I whisper.

"I have a heart that bleeds and beats only for you. My love for you knows no bounds."

A wave of contentment washes over my senses, and I exhale a happy sigh. Ash wraps his free arm around my back and pulls me into his chest.

Until this moment I never knew this kind of all-consuming love. It's a bone-deep emotion that radiates from my heart to the inner recesses of my soul. It's a connection that I can't get from anyone else and an unconditional sense of acceptance.

I don't care that Ash was a tree without money, resources, or status. Having him by my side is enough.

"Are you human, now?" I ask, still not quite believing what I'm seeing.

"A hybrid between species."

Ash releases my wrist and stretches out a hand. Green tendrils grow from his fingertips and sprout leaves.

I lace my fingers through his and gaze into his eyes, awestruck at his metamorphosis.

"You're beautiful," I whisper.

"Nowhere as beautiful as you," he says back.

I shift on my feet, my cheeks heating, and resist the urge to say something awkward. Ash has seen millions if not billions of creatures in his long existence. Who am I to second-guess his opinions?

"What happens now?" I ask. "Can you leave the forest?"

"I will go anywhere to be with you," he replies, "But first I want to know what it's like to kiss you in this form."

My lips part, and I tilt my head up to look him full in the face. The hunger in his eyes makes my heart race with anticipation. I want him just as urgently.

Ash leans in and presses his lips to mine, and a jolt of electricity races straight to my core. His tongue swipes against the seam of my mouth and I let him in. He still tastes of honey and maple syrup, but there's now a new flavor mixed in that's uniquely him. It's masculine, earthy, and makes my head spin.

I run my fingers through his hair, feeling wisps of silk, and slide my hands down soft skin encasing hard muscles. Everything about him is human, only fresher, newer, more perfect. It's as though he made this body only for me.

Ash pulls me closer, deepening the kiss, and I wrap an arm around his neck. My other hand explores his broad chest, tight abs, and the thick erection poking into my belly. The skin there is as velvety as rose petals encasing solid wood. I moan into his mouth, needing more.

As soon as my fingers close around his shaft, he eases me onto the ground. I land with my back sinking into a blanket of moss and gaze into his mesmerizing eyes.

They shimmer with flecks of amber and gold, reminding me of autumn leaves. His hair falls around his face, creating an effect that I can only describe as otherworldly.

"I love you," he says, pressing his lips to mine.

"I love you, too," I whisper into the kiss.

He draws back, his eyes darkening. Moonlight filters down through the canopy, which reveals glimpses of a starlit sky. I've had candle-lit dinners in some of the most romantic spots, but nothing compares to this.

Ash changed himself from a carnivorous tree that wanted to drain my blood and grind my corpse into plant food. He sacrificed his immortality to become a man so we could be together for the rest of our lives. Nothing could touch my heart so deeply.

"From this moment, I will never let you go," he rasps.

"Never," I murmur.

His lips crash onto mine for another kiss, this one rougher and more urgent. I wonder if he's thinking about my mortality because that's the only thing that could ever keep us apart.

"Milly, I can wait no longer," he says, his erection grinding into my belly. "I need to be inside you. Now."

Chapter Nineteen

Ash's words infuse my body with heat and desire. I gaze up into his darkening eyes, my heart melting under his gaze. All I ever wanted was another chance to see him and now he's turned himself into a man.

He brushes a strand of hair off my face, his touch lighting up my nerves with a surge of electricity. The attraction I have for him has surpassed the physical. He's burrowed deep into my heart and captured my soul.

"I need you inside me," I whisper, my voice trembling with anticipation.

Roots rise from beneath us and peel off my trench coat, leaving me lying in the maternity gown. The buttons pop as the plant fibers pull the fabric apart, leaving me bare.

Ash's gaze travels down my body, heating every inch of my skin. He pauses at my breasts, his lips parting. "What happened?"

"They captured me at the edge of the forest," I murmur. "One of their employees knocked me out, and I woke up being force-fed herbs to make me lactate."

Ash growls, his features twisting into a rictus of rage. "They died too quickly."

"It will wear off." I raise my fingers to his forehead and try to smooth out his brow. "I'm just glad they're gone."

"Is the younger man I killed your husband?" he growls.

A laugh bubbles up in my chest as I picture the weasel-faced man who offered me a ride back to the village, only to deliver me to the Freymans.

"What is so funny?" Ash asks.

"That was just the old man's assistant. My husband is still in the house."

"Good," he growls. "Because for every moment you endured with that wretched family, your husband will suffer a hundredfold."

Giddy warmth fills my chest, sending my butterflies into a tizzy of delight. Growing up with parents more interested in drugs than in their own child, it was rare for someone to feel outraged on my behalf, let alone rush to my defense. Now, I have a protector.

"You'd do that for me?" I ask, my voice breathy.

"I would drain every person in Scandinavia if it meant bringing you justice," he growls, his voice possessive and low. "You deserve the world."

He leans in, his lips brushing mine, and I arch into his touch. His kisses travel down my neck, over my collarbones, and toward my aching chest.

The lactation herbs and electronic pumps have left me so engorged with milk that my breasts are now tender and hot. I didn't notice the discomfort until the stress of the situation faded.

Now that my breasts are exposed to the elements, I'm acutely aware of their weight.

Ash lowers his head to my chest, his hand cradling my breasts as though they're as fragile as they feel.

"Do they hurt?" he asks.

"Yes," I whisper.

"I can prepare some willow bark for the pain and perhaps some cooling gel—"

"Are you allergic to strange herbs?"

He frowns. "Of course, not."

"Then suck my breasts," I rasp.

His gaze snaps to meet mine. "But the people I

killed imprisoned you to steal your milk. Now, you want me to do the same?"

"It's different," I reply.

"How?"

"They ache. I ache. Every part of me aches for your touch. Put my nipple in your mouth and draw out the milk."

He licks his lips, his gaze dropping back down to my breasts. "You should be warned that I will enjoy this."

A laugh bubbles from my chest. "That isn't exactly a surprise."

Ash trails soft kisses down one breast while cradling the other in his large hand. Cool liquid seeps from his palms, easing the intense heat. It feels a little like the substance he used on my flesh wound, only better.

He swirls his tongue around my aching nipple, infusing my skin with tingles.

"Fuck, Ash," I murmur, "That feels so good."

He takes my nipple into his mouth and slides his tongue up and down its peak with flicking and teasing strokes. I grind my hips against the erection pressing into my pussy and groan.

Ash has turned a situation I once found terrifying into something tantalizing. Now, I'm desperate for him to suck.

He draws on the nipple, his eyes fluttering shut with a moan. Each gentle pull sends jolts of pleasure to my aching clit. I buck against his erection, desperate for friction.

Sensation builds as he continues to drink. I arch and moan into his mouth, wanting him to go faster, harder, to take every drop.

Finally, he releases my nipple and gazes up at me, his eyes half-lidded, as though he's tipsy and content. "You taste even sweeter than I imagined."

"That was incredible," I say through panting breaths.

He licks his lips. "I want more."

"Take it."

He moves onto the other breast and sucks the nipple into his mouth. He licks and laps and gently latches, alternating between taking my milk and giving me pleasure.

"Please," I whisper. "I need to cum."

The erection pressing into my pussy changes shape, forming a tiny, wet opening that closes around my clit and sucks.

My breath catches. "Is that a mouth?"

"A knot," he replies around a mouthful of nipple. "Do you like it?"

The knot in his erection presses and pulls in unison with the mouth teasing my nipple. I close my eyes and drop my head back, my senses spinning with sublime sensations.

I've never imagined such pleasure, let alone experienced it, but he continues working my nipple and clit until I'm quivering. I never thought breastfeeding could be so pleasurable but this is the kind of intimacy I've craved. I'm so glad to be sharing it with him.

A tongue flickers out from the tiny mouth sucking at my clit, feeling so velvety that my legs tremble and my toes curl.

"What are you doing to me?" I cry.

"Making up for sending you away," he murmurs and swirls his tongue around my nipple. "I should have kept you safe. Protected you from harm."

The pleasure intensifies until my nerves are overwhelmed. Every lick, every flick, every pull on my nipple fills my core with molten ecstasy, while what he's doing to my clit keeps me teetering over a ledge.

All the discomfort I felt earlier is replaced by a different sort of ache. I'm aching with the onset of a powerful climax.

"Everything about you is beautiful," he mumbles around my nipple. "Your stories, your mind, your taste. You are more majestic than any creature in the forest, more nourishing than the earth, and shine brighter than the sun. I will never let you go."

I grip his shoulders and wrap my legs around his waist. "Fuck. I love you so much."

"I love you more," he growls.

His words push me over the edge. I climax with a rush of rapture and a long, breathy moan. Waves of pleasure crash through my senses, replacing my shock and terror with a deep sensation of bliss.

I'm twitching, trembling, tensing, and releasing, my pussy clamping and convulsing around nothing. Ash holds me close as the orgasm subsides, consenting to whisper words of love.

When my breathing calms and the spasms fade to gentle flutters, he pulls back and places a soft kiss on my lips.

My nostrils fill with the sweet scent of milk, and all I feel is warmth. Somewhere in the back of my mind is a tiny sense of loss.

Ash might look human, but he'll never give me a child. I'll never know what it's like to cradle my own baby. I push those thoughts to the recesses of my mind and focus on the afterglow.

"I'm so glad you found your way back to me," he murmurs. "When I traveled down to the well and found a way to be with you, I feared that you had already returned to England."

"Would you have come after me?" I whisper.

"I still don't know if I can even leave the forest,"

he replies, his eyes shining. "The plan was to capture a human and make him find a way to convince you to return."

A breeze rustles the overhead leaves, and moonlight shines down from the canopy, turning the ends of his hair an unusual shade of bronze. Ash looks like a nature spirit, a being of the highest magic.

I can't believe this awe-inspiring creature is in love with me.

"Those bastards didn't realize they were doing me a favor," I say. "Without them, I would never have met you."

Ash leans in for a kiss, his erection sliding against my wet core. "Thanks to the extra blood and the Well of Wisdom, I can now keep you by my side."

My lips curl into a smile. "I want us to make love under the stars."

He pulls back with a sharp grin. "I'll do one better."

"How?"

"I'm going to fuck you until you see stars."

Chapter Twenty

My breath catches, and my pussy throbs at the prospect of being filled. Ash draws back several inches, letting the roots that tore off my gown raise me off the ground.

"What are you doing?" I whisper.

"Taking you higher," he says. "I want to focus all my attention on you and not the predators prowling around to catch us off guard."

My gaze darts around the clearing, where I catch a few glimpses of glowing eyes. Some of them watch us through the bushes while others are higher up behind the smaller tree trunks.

"Oh," I whisper and glance around for signs of Clara and Peter. Mikael is already deep within the ground, hopefully, already consumed by the roots. "Where are the humans you killed?"

"Being pulverized into nutrients," Ash growls. "Enough about those bastards. Focus on getting fucked."

A cool breeze blows through the clearing, sending shivers skittering down my spine. I shift within my restraints, my body thrumming with need. The trees raise me toward the branches, which move apart to reveal more of the sky.

I glance down to see if Ash is standing on a platform, only to find his legs have lengthened like stilts.

"How are you doing that?" I whisper.

"You keep forgetting that I am a tree," he replies with a fond smile.

"But... But..." My gaze sweeps up and down his bare torso, taking in his broad shoulders, sculpted chest, and carved abs. "But you told me you were its heart."

He laughs as we rise above the branches, the sound deep and rich. "Look at it another way. Trees sometimes produce fruit."

"That's right?"

"Thanks to you, I've had a diet of blood and flesh and love. Combine that with the waters of the Well of Wisdom, and you have me."

My lips part. He could explain this over and over but I would still think it was magic.

"What I was before was a mere branch to the being I am today. Now, I am the fruit of your love."

Moonlight shines down on us from a cloudless indigo sky studded with twinkling stars. Tonight feels more special than all the times we had sex on the treetop because he's transcended from the mannequin that could only simulate a man. I finally have everything I ever desired. A companion whose heart connects with mine.

Ash stands between my spread legs, his skin glowing in the silver light. He's more than a man or a tree or a magical being—he's the rest of my life.

"That's... beautiful," I murmur. "You're beautiful."

The roots around my wrists and ankles snake down my limbs and meet at my back to form a platform to support my weight. My skin tingles. Ash is about to claim me under the stars.

His gaze softens. "I want to return the happiness you gave me a hundredfold. I want to spend the rest of our time together worshiping you like a goddess."

The words touch my heart like a caress, and I sigh. There's no time to bask in the implications of that promise because his fingers lengthen and split into thinner digits.

"What are you doing?" I whisper.

"Making sure to give every inch of your body the attention it deserves."

His fingers spread across my torso, some of them rolling my nipples, others stroking my skin. A set of digits make gentle flicking movements over my exposed clit. Sparks detonate across my nerve endings, making me gasp.

Pleasure radiates from his touch. I arch and twist within the fingers, my pussy clenching and releasing.

"You should see your cunt," he says, his voice breathy with awe. "It's dripping nearly as freely as your nipples."

"Oh fuck."

He has to be exaggerating. I want him to stick a finger in my pussy, but both his hands are already preoccupied

"Please, I can't take any more," I cry. "Just fuck me."

"Which hole?"

I raise my head and stare down past the mass of fingers branching over my body and to the thick erection standing to attention between my legs. Milky beads of precum gather on his slit before flowing freely down its shaft and disappearing into the branches.

"What did you say?" I ask through panting breaths.

"Choose a hole for me to fill," Ash replies.

"Pussy," I whisper.

"Are you sure about that?" he asks, his voice teasing.

There's no question about where I need him to fuck me but what if his cock can do the same as his fingers?

My tongue darts out to lick my dry lips. "Can you split your erection into two?"

"Of course," he replies.

"I mean, two equally as thick as your shaft."

His smile widens into a predatory grin. "Do you doubt me?"

The depth of his voice goes straight to my swollen clit, making me moan.

"No," I say through panting breaths. "Please, Ash. Fill both holes."

The fingers continue tweaking, stroking, sliding, and caressing my body. My toes curl and sweat breaks out across my brow, but I resist the urge to let my eyes roll to the back of my head. Ash is about to do something interesting with his cock—something I can't miss.

His huge penis expands to twice its usual girth, making my stomach drop. It's now thicker than the widest part of his forearm and looks like it would split me in half. My breath shallows, and I continue raising my head, desperate for what comes next.

"Are you ready?" he rumbles.

"Yes," I whisper. "Please."

He draws closer, his cock pressing down on my clit until I'm panting harder and faster than a hungry wolf. Then his slit opens up, letting out a stream of pearlescent fluid, and his entire head divides into two.

My lips part with a gasp, and I jerk forward, not quite believing my eyes. The split continues down his shaft, creating two fully formed erections that point to the left and right.

"Does that hurt?" I whisper.

"Mild growing pains," he replies with a smile. "But you're about to soothe the aches."

By the time his cock divides down to the base and forms two impressive-sized erections, my pussy is so hungry and wet that I'm no longer freaked out about his extra fingers or his duplicate cock.

"Give it to me," I whine. "Please."

Ash shifts his hips so one penis points toward my belly and the other lies flush against my asshole. He lines up the top penis to the entrance of my pussy and says, "Here it comes."

My legs tremble as he pushes the top erection inside. I'm so wet from earlier that he enters me with ease, even if there's still a delicious stretch. I gasp and clamp around the shaft, my asshole quivering in anticipation.

Ash's eyes widen, his face goes blank, and his body stiffens.

"What's wrong?" I ask.

"Fucking you with this cock is so much more sensitive than the one made of wood."

"What's it like?"

He groans. "Sweeter than drinking from the Well of Wisdom. More awe-inspiring than soaking in the magic from Asgard. Heavenly."

My eyes mist, and I exhale a shaky laugh. "Then keep going."

He thrusts, entering me to the hilt. With a moan, I clench around his shaft, feeling every vein and contour.

"Good girl," he says, his voice still breathy. "You took the first cock so well. Are you ready for the second?"

I give him an eager nod.

Warm, menthol-scented fluid oozes out of Ash's second cock, which I recognize as a lubricant he likes to use for anal sex. I'm already so attuned to it that my asshole relaxes enough to let him slide in.

"So tight," he says with a groan. "But just as magical."

Another giggle bubbles in my chest. No one has ever complimented me on my asshole.

Ash pulls back his hips and then drives back in, his dual cocks filling me beyond reason. Pleasure shoots through my insides, squeezing out a moan.

"Oh, god," I say.

"Wrong," he growls. "You are my goddess and I worship at your temples."

The roots tighten around my back and limbs to accommodate the force of his thrusts. Ash isn't being gentle by any means. We spent our week together exploring my limits and fucking until I cried for mercy. He knows exactly how much I can take.

Sex with Ash as a flesh and blood being is much more satisfying. His cocks are alive and no longer beautifully carved dildos and his body yields against mine. Even the way he gazes into my eyes as he pounds into me is different. It's like he's looking into my soul.

His handsome features contort instead of remaining artistically still, and my chest swells with pride. I know he loves me because of his sacrifice, but seeing his expressions make me truly feel like I'm affecting him on a level that's deeper than curiosity.

Waves of pleasure courses through my veins. I thrash within my restraints and squeeze around the dual cocks.

Ash hisses through bared teeth. "Here's another side effect of becoming almost human."

"What is it?"

"It's a battle not to spill in your tight holes."

"Fuck."

"Come for me," Ash says, his voice deepening several octaves.

My muscles clench and quiver with overwhelming ecstasy as Ash's movements quicken. He thrusts deeper and deeper, pushing me to the edge. The pleasure is all-consuming. It's exactly what I need. My mind tumbles backward into an abyss, my senses exploding into blissful release.

Ash's ragged breaths caress my neck, and he climaxes with a roar that makes my ears ring. Hot fluid spills into my spasming core, which seems to want to milk him of every drop.

After his last spurt, he collapses against my chest and breathes hard.

My restraints loosen a little, allowing me to relax into the afterglow. I'm not sure if it's because of the danger or the time we spent apart, but that was the best sex of my life.

"It's not enough," he rasps in my ear, his shaft already thickening and hardening, "I want to see how well you take another cock."

Chapter Twenty-One

Ash presses kisses on my lips as he expands the cock inside my pussy. The veins on his shaft double in size and push against my walls like fleshy branches.

I pant through the sensations, my heart thrumming as each extra inch pushes down on nerve endings that I barely knew existed.

The cock in my ass quivers as though considering doing the same, but I squeeze hard with my muscles, making him moan.

"Fuck, Milly," he growls into my ear. "You have no idea how good it feels to be encased in your love."

I shiver within my restraints as a set of tiny fingers make up-and-down strokes on my clit. "You know what?" I say between panting breaths. "If it's anything like taking your cocks then it must feel like heaven."

Ash's cock swells even further, stretching me until I ache. Sweat breaks out across my skin as the thick cock splits into two, which then twist and scissor within my pussy.

"Bloody hell," I cry, a fresh orgasm already building. "That feels amazing."

The dual cocks work in tandem, probing, pushing, and pressing down on my pleasure spots, while the one in my ass pistons in and out. Each of their movements propels me higher and higher until my entire body becomes a raw nerve.

"You look so beautiful, straining against my roots with your face twisted with ecstasy," Ash murmurs. "I would stay inside you like this forever, but we have one more task to complete."

"What...." One of his cocks drags against my G-spot and fills my vision with shooting stars. "What do you mean?"

"Later," he growls.

"Aahhh... Alright."

The digits rolling my clit are as small as my fingernails and switch to up and down strokes. Their pointed tips drag along my sensitive flesh, pushing me further until my lungs seize.

What is Ash doing to me? At this rate, I'm going to implode.

"Let go," he says, his voice coaxing. "You're completely safe."

My eyes widen. The sensations are so intense that I can't even breathe. "I-I—"

The fingers clamp around my clit and hold it like a vice, just as one of his cocks hits a spot that forces all the air out of my lungs.

An orgasm tears through me like a windstorm, picking up speed with the cocks' frantic movements. I thrash within my restraints, my body electrified with a current of pleasure. Ash holds me through the climax, and the roots tighten around my wrists and ankles to compensate. As soon as that orgasm fades, another takes its place.

"Good girl," Ash murmurs, his voice filled with admiration. "You're doing so well."

I'm so lost in the sensations that I can barely utter a response. All I can do is keep breathing as his fingers and cocks push me over one precipice after another.

Somewhere in the throes of my multiple orgasms, Ash bellows, the sound more intense than thunder. Hot fluid fills my holes, triggering yet another climax.

When I finally return to reality, my body is boneless and spent. Ash wraps his arms around me, and his roots lower me back to the forest floor.

"You were incredible," he murmurs, his voice filled with pride.

"So were you," I rasp.

He cradles my face with both hands and peppers kisses on my chin, my cheeks, and my lips. Each touch of his lips feels like a promise.

The floor softens, forming a thick mattress of moss, and brambles rise around us to create an enclosure. Starlight filters through the canopy, adding to the forest's magic.

"Not taking me back into the cavity?" I murmur.

"I want to experience my first night in this form outside the confines of my trunk."

Ash wraps his arms around my shoulders, drawing me to his chest. I nestle into his muscular body and relax to the steady rhythm of his heart.

As I drift off, something he mentioned earlier rises back to the surface.

"Which task were you talking about earlier?" I murmur.

"Your husband," he growls.

"Oh."

Now that I'm safe in Ash's embrace and nobody

wants to shoot me through the head or suck my nipples, I don't feel quite so murderous.

"What are you thinking?" I ask.

"He must pay for deceiving you."

"Don't kill him so soon. It would look suspicious if the entire family died and I was the only person to survive."

"I thought about that, too," he says.

My teeth worry at my bottom lip. I'm not normally so bloodthirsty but the sight of those guns triggered my survival instincts. There has to be a way to stop Erik without getting me into trouble.

"I learned something interesting in the Well of Wisdom," Ash says, his voice interrupting my thoughts. "There might just be a way for us to have a family."

Ash launches into stories about the Norse god of Mischief, who transformed into a mare, got pregnant, and gave birth to an eight-legged horse, followed by a description of the asexual reproduction of trees.

My eyelids droop. I force them open, but it feels like pushing lead weights. Sleep pulls at my consciousness, trying to drag me into the depths of slumber. My body relaxes, my breathing deepens, and my eyes pull shut.

"What are you saying?" I ask, the words slurred.

Ash kisses me on the forehead and murmurs, "Rest, my love. All will be clearer in the morning."

Hours later, Ash kisses me awake, and I open my eyes to find myself cradled in his arms at the edge of the forest. I glance over his shoulder for signs of the tree, but it's out of sight.

Morning sunlight shine through his long, chestnut-colored hair, accentuating the strong angles of his face. My fingers drift to his full lips that I want to spend the rest of my life kissing.

"You're real," I whisper.

"Did you think last night was a dream?"

"I still can't believe you're a separate, breathing being that can travel through the forest." My palm slides down to his chest, and I feel his steady heartbeat. "How are you feeling?"

"Small but surprisingly well, thanks to you and the recent sacrifices. Are you ready to begin our new life?"

"Yes," I whisper, my pulse quickening.

Ash sets me on my feet, and we walk naked, hand in hand until the trees thin and we reach the edge of the wildflower meadow that borders the Freyman farmhouse. It's a huge red monstrosity the exact shade of blood with white beams and window sills that remind me of milk.

My heart pounds, even though I know Ash has already killed most of Erik's family. There's a tiny part of me that associates this house with the trauma of deceit, the forced marriage, and being imprisoned and pumped full of lactation-inducing herbs.

Ash turns to me, his brow forming a deep V. "You are anxious."

"This place doesn't hold the best memories," I murmur.

"Then let us make better ones," he replies with a sharp grin.

A dark figure passes through an upstairs window, indicating that Erik has awoken. I used to wonder why a family as rich as the Freymans didn't have domestic servants but I doubt that they would want strangers reporting their antics to social media or the press.

Squeezing Ash's hand, I lead the way to the unlocked side door and slip into the boot room. Ash stares at wooden benches running down the length of the walls and the wooden coat hooks.

"Does it offend you that people cut down trees to make furniture?" I ask.

"All plants are living beings," he replies. "I understand the need to hunt for survival but there is no need to take the lives of trees when there is already so much fallen wood."

That pretty much sums up what I despise most about the family. It wasn't so much the adult breast-feeding but the coercion. Mikael could have paid someone to drink the herbs and provide him with milk but he was determined to take it by force.

We continue into a hallway of white walls and wooden floorboards and up the stairs. The portraits that once seemed majestic now fill me with revulsion.

How many of those intimidating-looking gentlemen preyed on innocent young women once their mothers could no longer provide them with milk? How many of women who refused their advances died?

We stop outside Erik's bedroom door. The muffled sound of singing tells me he's in the shower.

"Is that him?" Ash asks.

"Yes," I rasp.

Ash pushes open the door and steps inside. I walk in after him, my heartbeat echoing in my ears.

His room is empty, the bed unmade. As I flick my head toward the bathroom, the singing stops. A moment later, Erik emerges from the door, wet and naked, save for a towel around his hips.

Maybe it's the lack of breastmilk, but he looks pale and gaunt. He gapes at us, his eyes wide.

"Who the hell are you?" he asks Ash.

Ash steps forward, shielding me from Erik with his larger body. "I'm a man who has come to claim your wife."

"M-Milly?"

Erik steps back and grabs the door handle. Ash raises a hand and shoots a vine that wraps around my husband's neck. Erik falls to his knees with a harsh cry. Ash grabs his arm and drags him into the bathroom.

By the time I follow them in, Erik is standing naked in the shower with his arms pinned above his head. A vine encircles his wrists and keeps him in place, while a thick one wraps around his neck.

Erik turns to me, his eyes pleading. I advance toward him, but Ash holds out his arm. "If he tries to hurt you, he dies."

"Alright." I step back toward the door. Once I'm out of grabbing reach I ask Erik, "Why didn't you tell me the truth about your family before you proposed?

Erik swallows hard and hangs his head. "Who is this man?"

"Answer my question," I snap.

He flinches. "I'd tried being honest with different girls, but they were all disgusted," he says through sobs. "Then I tried setting my sights lower, choosing the ones that were less attractive, but even they rejected me."

My hackles rise at the implication that I'm even lower in his estimation than a woman he finds unattractive.

"So, you decided to lie?" I ask.

He struggles in Ash's grip, but the branches tighten, cutting off his air.

Erik's face turns a horrible shade of purple. "Even that didn't work. The last girl I married captured incriminating footage of us and threatened to post it online unless we released her with a huge payout."

"What happened to her?"

"She fell and broke her neck."

"You killed her?"

"Not me." Erik's voice rises several octaves. "My grandfather pushed her off the balcony. I'm just their pawn."

Ash and I exchange incredulous glances.

"I would believe you if you hadn't actively lured innocent women into your sick little world. If you didn't like what they were doing, you could have broken away from your family or refused to feed from your mother, but you didn't."

"Milly," he croaks. "Don't be silly. That would shorten my lifespan."

My nostrils flare. "You could have set me free, but you're the one who suggested the hunt and then taunted me when I got caught."

"Milly." Ash turns to me, his features grave.

"What?"

"Nothing you can say will make this man understand. He and his kind are a parasitic fungus that cannot be cured."

"You're right," I reply, my voice breaking. "I don't even know why I bothered to get him to admit that he was wrong."

"Are you going to kill me?" Erik rasps.

"We're going to keep you alive," I say.

Erik squeezes his eyes shut and collapses into his bindings.

"Don't feel relieved too soon," I add.

His eyes snap open. "What do you mean?"

"You're about to suffer the exact fate you set up for me."

Erik shakes his head. "I don't follow."

"You will in a moment."

Ash's cock rises to full mast and extends across the bath, making Erik thrash within his restraints.

"What are you doing?" he screeches.

"Hold still or you'll get hurt," I say.

"Please," he screams. "Don't do this."

I roll my eyes, pretty sure I said those words to him multiple times, only for him to laugh in my face and hurl insults.

Ash's cock forms a needle-sharp tip and pierces Erik through the balls.

"I thought you would skewer him through the stomach or groin," I murmur.

"My plan requires your husband's genetic material."

I lean against the bathroom door and watch. Erik's eyes roll to the back of his head, and he faints, giving Ash a moment to extract some semen and move the spike to Erik's abdomen.

"Will the baby be yours and Erik's?" I ask.

"And yours," Ash says with a smile. "You just released an unfertilized egg. I kept it safe and preserved it with my power."

"And you're sure it will work?"

He nods. "With a touch of my magic, the being I plant inside your husband will use his body as a host to incubate our offspring. When the time is right, it will break free."

The fine hairs on the back of my neck stand on

end. I should be horrified, but I can't bring myself to care. Escaping Erik and his family was never the answer. They would have used their vast resources to track me down wherever I hid and either bring me back to feed Mikael or secured my silence with my death.

Erik was already trawling the dating sites for another victim. Even with his family dead, I believe he would have continued his parasitic legacy.

Bright light emerges from the tip of Ash's pointed cock, which he sticks into Erik's belly button. Erik wakes up and screams.

"How long will the baby take to grow?" I shout over the sound of Erik's agony.

"A year, depending on how well the vessel is fed," Ash replies.

"Won't he run away and tell someone?"

"Once the being has taken hold, it will control the vessel's body until it is ready to emerge."

Light glows from within deep in Erik's belly, and Erik falls silent. He gazes at us through lifeless eyes, his lips parting with drool.

"What happens now?" I ask.

"In a few days, the being inside him will take control, and emulate your husband until it's time to emerge." Ash smiles. "Eventually, we will have a family."

I rise onto my tiptoes and throw my arms around Ash's neck.

The old wives' tale turned out to be bullshit. Getting my period on my wedding day gave me the best kind of luck. Not only did I tame a carnivorous tree, but I also destroyed a den of predators and found the love of my life.

Epilogue

ONE YEAR LATER.

I open the balcony's wooden door and step out into the elevated deck that runs along the perimeter of our log house.

Shortly after our baby gained consciousness and picked Erik's body off the floor, he set fire to the farmhouse and all its outbuildings.

It was the middle of the night, so none of the farm workers were there to put out the fire. By the time the police and fire department arrived, the entire farm had been razed to the ground. Using Erik's body as his puppet, our baby told the authorities we were camping in the forest, only to return to find his ancestral home ablaze.

They believed his lie, and we hosted one big

memorial service for his newly deceased parents and grandparents. It was even more impressive than the wedding.

I continue through the deck to find Ash standing over a hammock made of his vines. He and the baby designed it out of saplings from the original ash tree, which they bent and twisted to form a structure made of living wood.

"This is where you're hiding?" I ask.

He turns to me and smiles. "I was going to nudge you with a branch when the time was right."

"What are you talking about?"

A deep groan turns my attention to the hammock.

Erik lies within its depths, his features twisted in agony. My gaze darts to Ash.

"Is something wrong with the baby?"

"That's your husband."

"He's not—" I shake my head. "What's happening?"

"The baby wants to be born."

My jaw drops. "Already?"

Erik cuts us off with a groan. "Milly, help me."

"What's the baby doing?" I ask. "Can you communicate with him?"

Ash wraps an arm around my shoulders and

pulls me into his larger body. "He's clever enough to release control of a body that's in pain."

I place a hand on my chest and exhale a long sigh. "Thank goodness. I can't wait to see what he's like."

Erik's screams are loud enough to wake the dead. I'm thankful that Ash planted a wide ring of trees around our property to safeguard our privacy. Thanks to these extensions of his original body, we've caught predators, nosey reporters, and distant relatives eager to get their claws into the family business.

Our baby's control of Erik's body hasn't been absolute. Every so often, Erik's consciousness pushes through and he screams for help. I've always been at his side to gaslight everyone else into believing that he's still traumatized by the fire.

Light shines from Erik's rounded stomach, along with buckets of fluid. He thrashes within the hammock, rocking it to the side, but a slew of branches wrap around his limbs like constrictors.

My pulse quickens, my breath shallows, and I wait for the baby to appear.

"Does he need help?" I ask.

Ash tightens his grip on my shoulder. "Think of this process like shoots breaking through the soil and reaching for the sun."

"Alright," I whisper.

Moments later, a tiny hand pushes its way through his belly. I step forward, eager for a closer look. Another hand appears, followed by a head with a full head of wet, dark hair.

"You're here," I whisper, my fingers itching to scoop up our baby.

It takes every ounce of self-control to remain in place as the baby's face emerges from Erik's belly. Nothing about his features says he's part plant. Round cheeks, a snub nose, and huge, dark eyes.

He's perfect.

Ash's breath catches, and he steps forward and hovers his hands over the baby's head. The baby's face turns upward the way some flowers bask in the sun, and he reaches up with a tiny hand to grasp Ash's finger.

I love him already.

The baby turns to scan my face and stretches out a hand. I step forward and offer him my finger.

"Can you talk?" I ask.

He shakes his head no.

"He wants you to know that his vocal cords are still developing but he will find a way to communicate."

I nod, my eyes misting. "Can I hold you?"

The baby releases Ash's finger and offers me his

other hand in the universal sign children make that means 'pick me up.'

I take him in my arms and cradle him to my chest. The tiny heartbeat reverberating in my palms is strong and steady.

He's mine.

Ash wraps his arms around my shoulders and pulls us both into an embrace. He presses a kiss on the baby's head and murmurs, "Welcome to the family, little one."

The baby tilts his head back and offers us both a gummy smile.

"Have you chosen a name yet?" I ask, my voice breathy with awe.

He nods and turns to Ash.

"Magni," Ash says. "Named after the son of Thor."

"Welcome to the world, little Magni," I murmur into his head.

Magni cuddles into my chest and closes his eyes, his little body radiating joy. After setting the farmhouse on fire, he lay dormant for most of his gestation period, only awakening on the occasions we needed Erik to speak to someone on our behalf. I can't wait to get to know him.

A pained groan sounds from the hammock. I

turn to find another hand reaching out through the hole in Erik's belly.

"Twins?" I ask.

Ash chuckles. "Surprise."

I whirl on him, my eyes wide. "You knew all along that there were two?"

"I fertilized and planted two eggs but I wasn't sure if they would both survive." He presses a kiss on my temple. "Forgive me, Milly, but I couldn't stand for you to endure even more heartache."

My heart melts, and I gaze down at the baby emerging from Erik's belly. The second infant is smaller than Magni, with blond curls and bright blue eyes.

"Those are Erik's features," I murmur.

Ash hovers his hands over the baby, who gazes up at him with a serene smile.

"She needs a little more attention," Ash says, his voice gruff. "Erik's body tried its best but it wasn't cut out to sustain two lives."

My chest fills with joy, and tears gather in my eyes. I haven't felt such happiness since Ash emerged from the tree as a man.

"A daughter?" I ask with a sob.

"Our little princess," Ash replies with a smile.

Erik groans, and his body falls slack.

"What's happening?" I whisper.

"He passed out."

"Will he survive?"

Ash pulls our daughter out of Erik's belly, which closes with a snap.

"I'll give him enough nutrients to sign all the official paperwork and appoint the children as his heirs. After that, he'll check into a hospital, succumb to his disease, and die."

"That reminds me. What about their family's condition. Do the babies have it?"

"Certainly not," Ash replies. "They aren't' even fully human."

Relief floods my system. I lean into Ash's side and kiss our daughter on the head. "Welcome to our family," I murmur. "Have you decided on a name?"

Ash's laugh makes my skin tingle. "She wants to be called Loki."

I gaze down into her mischievous blue eyes and smile.

Last year, I was running for my life. Now, I have a soulmate and two miracle babies—a family worth killing for.

Karma works in mysterious ways.

About the Author

I write dark contemporary and paranormal romance featuring villains, monsters, morally gray heroes, and the women who make them feral.

When I'm not writing steamy scenes, you'll probably find me at my TikTok, @SiggyShade

Join my newsletter for exclusive short stories and updates on upcoming books: www.siggyshade.com/newsletter

Also by Siggy Shade

Paranormal Romance:

Tentacle Entanglement

Jack's Head

Stalked by the Boogie Man

Birched by the Krampus

Breeding with Bigfoot

Swallowing Water

The Loch Ness Monster

Contemporary Romance

Wicked Lessons

Manacled to Medicine

Dance for Daddy

Dinner with Daddy

Breed for the Beast

Printed in Great Britain
by Amazon

56848746R00139